Shotgun Messenger

The outlaws' first mistake was shooting the dog. That dog belonged to Rhett Coulter and he wasn't a man to mess with, as Lorne Roberts and his gang of gunslicks would soon discover.

Meanwhile, Coulter's friend's ranch, the Block H, is burned down and his woman barely escapes with her life. Now he has another reason to want to put Roberts out of business, quite apart from the little matter of his hoard of stolen bullion.

As Coulter fights against overwhelming odds, events hurtle along like a runaway stagecoach towards the final, blistering showdown. . . .

By the same author

Pack Rat
Coyote Falls

Shotgun Messenger

Colin Bainbridge

ROBERT HALE · LONDON

First published in Great Britain 2011

ISBN 978-0-7090-9091-5

Robert Hale Limited
Clerkenwell House
Clerkenwell Green
London EC1R 0HT

www.halebooks.com

Typeset by
Derek Doyle & Associates, Shaw Heath
Printed and bound in Great Britain by
CPI Antony Rowe, Chippenham and Eastbourne

CHAPTER ONE

OK, so it was only a dog. Trouble for Bayard – and Roberts – was, it was Coulter's dog.

Coulter had gone into Lone Creek for supplies while Bragg carried on panning in the river upstream of where they usually worked when the dog started growling. They both trusted that animal. If he was growling it was for a reason, and it soon became obvious when five mean-looking *hombres* came riding by.

'Which way to Lodesville?' the leader asked.

Bragg told them it was about twenty miles away, down from the hills.

'We're lookin' for a man called Reber. Know the name?'

Bragg was eyeing the gang all this time. They were carrying quite a weight of artillery among them. Bragg had left his gun behind. It wouldn't have made any difference with these gentlemen.

'I said we're lookin' for a man called Reber.'

'I heard you.'

'When I ask a question I expect an answer.'

One of the other men cut in. 'Leave it, Bayard.'

'You've had all the answer you're goin' to get.' Bragg turned away and the next instant a shot rang out, splashing up water an inch from his boots. Before Bragg could respond the dog suddenly leaped forward and launched himself at the gunman. The man's horse reared up as the dog's teeth fixed themselves into his leg. He let out a howl of pain as he struggled to gain control of the horse. Shaking the dog free, he swung his revolver round and shot it at close range. The dog let out one whimper and then lay on the ground. Bragg flung himself at the gunman, but a second shot creased his temple and he didn't know anything else till he came round later. The first thing he did was examine the dog. It was dead. Then he made for the stream to bathe his forehead from which blood was flowing. His head hurt and he feared that he might have been badly hit but it turned out to be only a deep graze. Another fraction of an inch and his skull would have been blown away. He was about to step out of the water and make his way back to camp when he passed out again.

Coming back from town with the supplies, Coulter unloaded them before gathering his equipment and making his way upstream to where he knew Bragg would be working. He saw the big man straight away but not the dog. Bragg was lying partly in and partly out of the water. He pulled him to the bank and dressed the wound as best he could. He was relieved when Bragg's eyes opened.

'What happened?' Coulter asked.

Bragg blinked and shook his head. He was suffering from concussion and his recollection for a moment was hazy. Then he remembered the dog.

'Pecos,' he said. 'They killed Pecos.'

Coulter's face was grim. Without waiting to hear Bragg's story he sprang to his feet and looked about. It didn't take him long to see the dog. With a few strides he had reached the dead animal and lifted it in his arms. For a few moments he remained that way until he was joined by Bragg. Briefly the wounded man outlined what had happened. When he had finished Coulter began walking with the dog in his arms. When they got back to the camp he laid it down, went into the tent and emerged with a shovel and a piece of wood. He walked to a grassy spot a hundred yards away from the camp and, placing the dog on the ground, began to dig. Bragg made to help him but then stopped. He figured it would be better to let Coulter get on with it. It didn't take long before Coulter had dug a deep enough pit to receive the body and provide it with protection from the wolves. Picking up the dog, he laid it gently in the earth. He began to shovel again, tipping the soil over the dog's remains. When he had finished he took up the wooden board and with a knife began to notch it. It took some time. When he had finished he stood the board up and secured it with earth and stones so that it stood solidly upright. The board read:

Pecos. A good dog and an old friend.
Gone to the diggin's.

For a few moments he stood with his hat in his hands looking at the sign. Then he turned to Bragg.

'We weren't doin' much good here anyways,' he said.

'Nope, place seems plumb worked out.'

'Then let's head for Lodesville. Maybe we'll pick up somethin' there.' Coulter made towards the tent before turning back to Bragg. 'How's the head?'

'It'll be fine once I'm in the saddle,' he said.

A pale ghost of a smile flickered across Coulter's features.

'What was the name of that *hombre* they was askin' for?'

'Reber,' Bragg replied. 'And the varmint who shot Pecos is called Bayard.'

Coulter nodded. 'That gives us plenty to go on,' he said.

It didn't take long for them to strike camp. They reloaded the wagon with the supplies Coulter had bought in town and stacked their equipment alongside. There wasn't much of it. Coulter hadn't been merely rhetorical when he said they hadn't been doing much good: it was the simple truth. Both of them knew they weren't really cut out to be prospectors. As they travelled in the wagon down the trail from the hills, their saddle horses tethered behind, they went past some of their counterparts. At the water's edge men were working hard, dipping metal bowls into the sand and gravel of the river-bed, taking bowls out of the placer and swirling them around, gradually emptying out the sand and water. Other men, some of them in little groups, were making use of a rocker to try and extract any particles of gold, pouring water on to the dirt from the river in a sieve. At a spot where a tributary stream flowed into the river from a higher level a further group was gathered round a series of troughs into which some men were shovelling dirt while others stirred it up. The finer sand sieved through, catching any gold against the cleats.

'Howdy!' Coulter said, drawing the wagon to a halt. 'Any of you seen a gang of riders pass this way?'

One of the prospectors came forward. He glanced briefly into the wagon.

'You boys leavin'?' he said.

'Things just changed,' Coulter replied.

The man looked up at the two of them seated on the wagon box.

'Sorry I can't help you,' he said. 'Ain't seen no riders.'

'Look out in case they come by,' Coulter said.

The man hesitated. 'Where's the dog?' he asked.

'He's up there lookin' for the motherlode.'

When they arrived in Lone Creek they made for the livery stable where they arranged to leave the wagon and the mules. The ostler raised some objections but his concerns were soon put to rest by the sight of a roll of dollar bills.

'Matter of interest,' Coulter said, 'you haven't noticed any strangers in town?'

'Strangers?' the ostler replied.

'Gunslicks. Five of 'em, maybe more.'

The ostler paused for a moment. He was thinking about those dollar bills. He obviously decided that honesty, in this case, was the best policy.

'Nope,' he said. 'Less'n they overlooked the livery stables.'

Coulter pressed another note into his hand anyway. 'Make sure you keep those mules well fed,' he concluded.

When they had settled with the ostler they stepped into leather and rode out of town. It was only a small burg. Lodesville was bigger but not too big. It shouldn't take them long to locate the riders if that was indeed where they were heading.

Night came down and they continued riding till the early hours. They reckoned they must be pretty close to Lodesville but needed some rest. They didn't bother building a fire. As soon as they lay down they were asleep. When dawn began to lighten the horizon they quickly ate some jerky before mounting up and riding on. It was further to Lodesville than they had allowed for and afternoon had arrived before they saw the town ahead of them. It was clear that something was happening. From further back along the trail they had heard church bells ringing and, as they moved closer, they could see that there were a lot more people on the streets than would be normal. Turning down a side street, they tethered their horses to a hitch rack and returned to the main drag. Coming down the dusty street was a hearse drawn by horses with black plumes, followed by a small procession of people. Mingling with the crowd, they followed the hearse. Moving very slowly it made its way down the length of the street, across a tree-lined square at the centre of the town and along another street on the far side. Soon it arrived at the town cemetery. The hearse came to a stop and four men stepped forward. Carefully they slid a coffin out of the hearse and, each of them taking a corner, carried it to an open grave which had clearly been recently dug. The people gathered round as a figure in black stepped forward. It was the reverend. The men carrying the coffin placed it down and then it was lowered into the ground. The people had all gathered as close to the grave as they could. They made up a considerable crowd and it was evident that whoever was being buried was held in high regard by the townsfolk. Coulter and Bragg stood towards the back of the crowd, but the preacher spoke in a loud voice and his words were carried to them on the breeze.

'We all owe something to Rance Germain. Without him this town would never have survived. When things were almost out of hand he took it by the scruff of the neck and cleaned it of the vermin that would have destroyed it. Now he is gone, taken by the same scourge he once cleared.'

Coulter looked at his companion. 'This Germain,' he whispered. 'Looks like somebody killed him but it couldn't have been the varmints we're lookin' for. The townsfolk wouldn't have had no time to organize this.'

The words of the preacher still reached their ears in scraps as they turned and started walking away.

'Man is but grass – gathered unto the harvest—'

They made their way back to the main street and entered an eating-house. There was a sign over the door: *June's Restaurant and Boarding-house.* The place was quiet. Behind the counter stood a well-built woman of about forty with long, greying hair.

'Good afternoon, gentlemen,' she said.

They sat by the window at a table with a blue checked cloth and a faded flower in a glass jar.

'Afternoon, ma'am. What have you got?'

'Looks like you boys could do with a good feed. I could do you bacon, beans, eggs, hash browns, grits.'

'And coffee,' Coulter said.

'Comin' right up.' Giving them a smile, she disappeared behind a bead curtain at the back of the counter.

'A fine-lookin' woman,' Bragg commented. 'Guess she must be the proprietor.'

Coulter glanced through the window. The street was quiet. Presently the woman reappeared with two steaming platters. She set them down, went out again and quickly reappeared with a pot of coffee. She poured out two mugs of the steaming thick liquid.

'Don't think I've seen you boys round town,' she said.

'Just passin' through,' Coulter said.

'Been workin' the hills?'

Bragg looked at her.

'I can spot the signs,' she said. 'I guess you didn't have no luck.'

Coulter took a long sup of the coffee. It tasted good.

'Seems like we come at an awkward time,' he said.

'You mean the buryin''?'

'Yeah. Seems like whoever it was they were puttin' in the ground was a popular man. There was a good number of townsfolk up there on the hill. Seems like they owed him a lot of respect.'

She shrugged and made a sound like a snort. 'Pity

they couldn't have shown it when he was still alive.'

Bragg wiped the corner of his mouth.

'If you don't mind us askin',' he said, 'but what's the story?'

She paused for a moment or two, as if sizing them up. Then she pulled out a chair and sat beside them.

'Why should I mind?' she said. 'It's simple. Rance Germain was town marshal. When he first came here the place was goin' to the dogs. He tamed the place, made it a decent town for folks to live in. Trouble is, people forgot how it was. There hadn't been trouble in a long time. Then, about five days ago, a bunch of no-goods come driftin' through. Caused a heap of trouble. Rance hadn't had to strap on his guns for ages. He confronted them in Hatch's Saloon when they started smashing up the place. He didn't have a chance.'

'Nobody backed him up?' Coulter said.

'They're makin' a big thing out of it now,' she replied. 'Buildin' him up an' all. But not one of them was there when he needed it.'

'So what happened to his killers? How many of them were there?'

'There was a bunch of 'em. It was nothin' to them. After they shot him they just finished up havin' their fun and then rode out again. Nobody had the nerve to try and do anythin'. They just skulked away and then come crawlin' out again when the shootin' and the high jinks was over.'

'Sounds like you ain't got a high opinion of them.'

'I don't have any opinion of 'em or the town. Rance was the only decent man among them.'

'You say this happened a few days ago. You ain't seen anythin' of those riders since?'

'Nope. Why do you ask?'

'Because I figure they're the same bunch come ridin' up to our camp and shot my dog. They asked my partner here if he knew of a man called Reber.'

The woman snapped to attention. 'Reber?' she said. 'Why, that was the name of one of those no-good coyotes. A couple of them came right in here. One of them called the other by that name. It's unusual so I wasn't likely to forget it.'

'What did he look like?'

'I wasn't likely to forget that either. Short man, looked like a polecat. You know what I mean?'

Coulter nodded. 'Sure, I know what you mean.'

'Sorta short in the legs and slim in the body,' she continued. 'Smelt a bit like one too.'

Coulter and Bragg had finished eating. They stood up and Coulter produced a wad of notes from his pocket.

'That was some meal,' Coulter said. 'Be good to have you in charge of the chuck wagon.'

'Any time,' she said. She went behind the desk to get their change.

'You boys plan on stayin' around for long?'

Coulter and Bragg exchanged glances.

'Ain't rightly sure,' Coulter said.

'You could put up here if you like. For as long as you like. Don't make no difference to me if it's one day or one month. Terms is good.'

'If they're anythin' like the cookin' they'll do fine. You know, we just up and left what we were doin'. Didn't give it a lot of thought. Might be an idea to stick around for a few days.'

'Good,' she said. 'Let me show you your rooms. Name's June, like it says on the board. June Campbell.'

'Rhett Coulter and Denver Bragg.'

She looked closely at Bragg. 'He don't say a lot,' she added.

When they had seen the rooms and pocketed the keys, Coulter and Bragg collected their horses and made their way to the livery stables to leave them.

'How long for?' the ostler said.

'Ain't sure.'

Again Coulter pulled out the wad of notes and with a feeling of *déjà vu* advised the man to keep them well fed and groomed. As they were about to leave he turned back to the ostler.

'Bad luck about the marshal,' he said.

The man looked at him suspiciously.

'We was at the burial,' Coulter added.

'Yeah? I would have been there myself, but I had business.'

'What happened?'

'I don't know. Seems like the marshal got involved in some sort of altercation.'

'Who with?'

'Like I say, I don't know nothin'. I wasn't there.'

'Guess you had some business, eh?' Coulter commented.

They emerged from the gloomy interior of the livery stables into the harsh light of day.

'Reckon I'm for a bath and a haircut,' Coulter said. 'How about you?'

'Maybe later,' Bragg replied.

Coulter knew better than to take it further. He crossed the street to the barber shop while Bragg headed for Hatch's Saloon.

When he arrived at the bar the bartender greeted him by placing a bottle and glasses in front of him. In the middle of the room a roulette wheel spun and a couple of men took their places, a pile of celluloid chips stacked beside them in cylinders of red, white and blue. At a table in a corner of the room a game of monte was in progress. The men pulled up chairs. No one spoke but made signs when they chose to pass and watched the dealer closely through the haze of tobacco smoke that filled the air. Painted women hovered about to distract the players. The game started small but they were soon playing for higher stakes. A group of three men came through the batwings and planted their boot heels on the brass rail. Bragg looked up. One of them he recognized; it was one of the men he had encountered at the river. All three of them looked like trouble. The game of monte was becoming more serious and suddenly there was tension in the air. One of the players wearing a new silk shirt and new boots with five-pointed stars stitched in them, was losing quite heavily and another of the players was insisting on higher and higher stakes to which the dealer eventually objected. The player tried to get him to increase his limit, and when the dealer refused, called to one of the three men who had just entered the room and was standing at the bar. The man Bragg recognized came across.

'Hey, Asa,' the player said. 'How about one of you taking my overbets?'

The man nodded towards his companions at the bar and one of them made to come over to join him. Before he could do anything, Bragg stepped forward.

'I'll take all bets above the sums you want,' he said, addressing the dealer.

The dealer wasn't happy with this arrangement, but the situation did not seem propitious for him to voice his reservations. Everyone in the saloon was watching now as Bragg pulled up a chair and joined the group round the table. The cards were dealt and soon Bragg was winning. When he had won above $500, he tipped the chair aside and rose to leave. He strolled over to the bar and ordered drinks for the onlookers. Then he turned to go. Before he reached the batwings the gunslick's voice rasped out, 'Where's that share of the winnings you promised me?'

Bragg stopped and then turned. 'I promised you nothing,' he said.

'That's not the way we saw it, is it, boys?' the man responded, addressing his friends at the bar. He had obviously failed to recognize Bragg.

'Sure isn't,' one of them said.

'Seems like I heard you promise him half the winnin's.'

'If you're calling me a liar,' Bragg responded, 'you'd better be ready to back it up.'

Surreptitiously, people began to move. The bartender started to reach for something under the counter but thought better of it and backed away. Bragg's features were tempered steel. His eyes were steady and remote, like water in cold moonlight. A moment passed that seemed to hang suspended and then the man called Asa reached for his gun. Before his hand had touched his gun handle Bragg's gun was belching fire and smoke. Blood sprang from the man's chest and he went backwards across the card table, bringing it down with him in a crash of splintering wood. In the same instance Bragg had swivelled and fired two more slugs into one of the men at the bar. The man stood for a second with a look of disbelief on his countenance, took one step forward, and then dropped forward like a felled tree.

Bragg hurled himself sideways as the third man fired, rolling over as he hit the floor. Taking a fraction of a second to steady himself, he fired again and the man's head seemed to explode as Ray's bullet caught him under the chin and exited through his skull, ricocheting from the wall behind. Bragg got to his feet. The air was heavy with smoke and the smell of gunpowder and the onlookers' ears were ringing with the deafening blast of the gunfire.

Bragg put his gun back into its holster.

'If there's any law, tell him he can find me at June's boarding-house,' he said. Turning, he walked out slowly. The batwings swung.

'Better get the undertaker,' the barman said.

A few men carried the bodies through to a back room. The swamper appeared with a bucket of sand and a broom. The roulette wheel began to hum and the card players resumed their seats at the table. Monte was being dealt.

Bragg made his way back to the boarding-house. Climbing to his room, he hung his holsters over the bedpost and lay down on the bed. It wasn't long before he heard footsteps on the stairs and then there came a knocking on the door.

'Are you in there, Mr Bragg?' It was June Campbell.

'Sorry to disturb you, but I got the new marshal here. He wants to speak with you.'

'Door's not locked,' Bragg called.

The door opened and June appeared accompanied by a tall, cadaverous individual wearing a tin star on his shirt.

'Didn't take you long to get here,' Bragg said.

The marshal suddenly pulled out his gun. Bragg's glance sped to his gunbelt, but it was just out of reach.

'I don't want no trouble,' the marshal said. 'Get up real slow and come with me.'

'What'd I do?' Bragg said.

'Killed three men. I just come from Hatch's.'

'Ask anyone there,' Bragg replied. 'They'll tell you how it was.'

'This is a peaceful town. We don't like strangers stirrin' up trouble.'

'That what you said to those boys shot up Rance Germain? Didn't take you long to pin that badge on yourself.'

'I ain't arguin' with you. It's just a question of whether you accompany me to the jailhouse or whether I have to shoot you for tryin' to escape.'

Bragg glanced towards June. There was a look on her face he couldn't quite decipher.

'OK,' he said, 'put the gun away. I don't want to cause no difficulties for the lady.' He got to his feet and moved to the door. The marshal's gun was still in his hand and Bragg felt it pressed against his spine.

'There's no need for that,' June commented. 'He said he was comin' peaceful.'

The marshal pushed the gun hard into Bragg's back.

'Start walkin',' he snapped.

They went down the stairs and into the street which was strangely empty. The marshal and Bragg continued walking while June remained behind observing their progress. The marshal's office was a low brick-built building. Behind it were two empty cells. Thrusting Bragg into one of them, the marshal locked the door.

'Enjoy your stay,' he said, and walked down the interconnecting passage to his office where he shut the door and sat at his desk, his legs propped up on the table. After a while he opened a drawer and pulling out a bottle of whiskey, poured himself a stiff drink.

Bragg looked around him. The cell was small and admitted light through a high barred window. Bending his knees, he slid to the floor and started to think about the situation. He had no regrets about having exacted vengeance on the men who had been involved in killing Coulter's dog. In a way he had set them up, but he had given them a fair chance – more than a fair chance since they had been three against one in the shootout. What he wasn't sure about was how to take the new marshal. He seemed to have taken on the role very quickly. Had the townsfolk had any say in the appointment or had he just assumed the position? Most likely he had been installed as the front man for some operation. If so, Bragg didn't rate his chances of getting out of jail very quickly. It didn't concern him unduly. Coulter would soon know about what had happened. He would do something about it. After a time he heard the outer door slam. The marshal had left.

The cell was naturally gloomy and as night approached it got darker. Bragg was thankful that he had eaten well at June's restaurant. Even so he was beginning to feel hungry but there was nothing he could do but await the coming of day. The night seemed endless. After a time he began to feel cold. Yet eventually the black night gradually gave way to the approach of dawn. Sounds began to infiltrate the silence of the cell – the shrill of a bird and the distant barking of a dog. Suddenly he tensed. He thought he heard a sound – not a bird or a dog this time, but a muted footfall. He listened as carefully as possible. He could not be certain, but he thought he heard it again. Then his ears picked up another sound – a low whisper. He strained to look up at the barred window frame. It came again, barely audible, the hushed sound of someone saying his name.

'Denver, Denver.'

He couldn't be certain who it was out there. Maybe it was some trick being played on him.

'Bragg,' the voice continued, 'it's Coulter. We'll get you out of there. Just leave it to us.'

Bragg had been lying on the floor. Now he quickly

got to his feet. He knew Coulter would do something, but what did he mean by 'us'? The whispering came again, this time slightly louder. The window was suddenly obscured.

'Roll away from the window. We're going to try pulling out the bars.'

Bragg could just make out fingers fastening a rope around the bars. It was high up – he guessed that Coulter was standing on something, probably a horse. If so, Bragg could only hope that the animal would not make any noise to betray its presence. He need not have worried. The face at the window disappeared. For a matter of moments the quietness continued before shattering in a sudden outburst of sound. From further away came the crackle of gunfire and, at the same moment, a shout from close at hand. The rope around the window bars tautened. There was a moment of tension, and then the bars came away, pulling a good section of the brick wall away with them in the process. Bragg spluttered as a cloud of dust enveloped him, and then the figure of Coulter appeared at the opening, climbing over the debris.

'There's a horse outside,' he snapped. 'Get into the saddle and ride.'

The gunshots had ceased. The place seemed oddly quiet again. Bragg was stamping and swinging his arms, trying to restore his circulation. Coulter grabbed him and helped him to climb over what was left of the wall. A horse stood outside; someone was busy unfastening the rope which had been used to pull out the window bars from the cantle of its saddle. A little way off he could see two other horses. He stopped, confused. Then he saw that the figure by the horse was June Campbell.

'What the hell. . . ?' he began, but the voice of Coulter behind him urging him to get moving put a stop to any further questions. Running to one of the horses, he leaped into the saddle. Coulter was right behind him and then the three of them were off at a gallop. As they thundered down the empty streets someone began to shoot, but there was little chance of them being hit. Only once Coulter turned in the saddle and fired back, but it was a token gesture. Their horses' hoofs echoed eerily from the false-fronted buildings and soon they were out of town, riding hard across the landscape. The night was still dark but to the east the sky was tinged with the first pale rays of dawn. Gradually, confident that no one was following them, they slowed to a steady trot and then finally they stopped.

'Appreciate you gettin' me out,' Bragg said.

'Yeah. You should have come to the barber's with me. It would've made things a whole lot easier.'

'I recognized one of the *hombres*. He was with the varmint who shot Pecos. He was in the bar with a couple of his gunslick friends.'

Coulter's features registered the faintest look of surprise.

'Wish I'd been there,' he said. 'You should have left him for me.'

'There's the rest of 'em. In fact, I reckon there's a whole nest of the varmints just waitin' to be smoked out. The ones back at the diggin's were just some of 'em. I figure they were meetin' up with others.'

'The ones who shot Germain?'

'Yeah.'

Bragg looked from Coulter to June Campbell. 'I figured Coulter'd be stoppin' by,' he said, 'but if you don't mind me askin', what are you doin' here?'

A grin spread itself across the woman's features.

'A good question,' she said. 'You know, I just ain't so sure myself.'

'Sorry to have got you involved.'

Her grin became a rippling laugh. 'Hell,' she said. 'Like I told you, boys, I've had enough of that low-down town. I never realized just how much till Rance Germain got killed and no one stood by him. I reckon you two comin' by is just about the best thing that could've happened.'

'What about the café?' Coulter said.

'My cousin Clara will look after it. She always hankered after takin' a share.'

'It's not too late to go back. Nobody would have recognized you.'

'What about whoever was doin' the shootin'?' Bragg asked.

'Whoever it was, he was a long ways off. It was dark.

He couldn't have known who was involved.'

'No point in arguin' about it,' June said. 'Fact is, I don't intend goin' back. That is, if you two are OK about havin' me ride along?'

Coulter and Bragg exchanged glances.

'We'd be right honoured,' Coulter said. Reaching into his saddle-bags he produced Bragg's gunbelt and guns.

'There was this too,' he said, handing Bragg a bundle of notes. 'Your winnin's from the saloon.'

Bragg laughed. 'Guess there's nothin' stoppin' us now,' he said. 'We even got the funds.'

In the cold light of dawn they all looked at each other.

'Not sure exactly for what,' Coulter said. 'But I guess we'll soon be findin' out.'

CHAPTER TWO

They carried on riding till they reckoned to have put sufficient distance between themselves and Lodesville. Riding up into some rocks they dismounted and having first attended to the horses, set about making a noon camp. They were quite well provisioned. Between them, Coulter and June Campbell had planned things well. June soon had a good meal prepared and while they ate they continued to discuss the situation.

'Are you sure you don't just want to go back to Lodesville?' Coulter asked June. 'I figure that new marshal is a crook, but the fact still remains we're now outside the law.'

'Git some coffee down you and stop talkin' nonsense,' June replied. 'I'm just beginnin' to enjoy myself.'

'Well,' Coulter continued, 'don't say you didn't know the situation.'

'Figure they'll come lookin' for us?' Bragg said.

'Yup. The marshal's probably roundin' up a posse right now. He'll figure to make a name for himself. Besides which, whoever is behind him won't be content to just let pass what happened in Hatch's Saloon. Whatever they're up to, they'll reckon it might be wise to have us out of the way. From what June says, they don't seem likely to have much opposition from the rest of the townsfolk.'

'So what's goin' on?' Bragg said.

Coulter turned to June. 'You know this place,' he said. 'Any ideas why those gunslicks seem to have singled out Lodesville?'

June forked some beans into her mouth before replying, 'Could be they just rode this way by chance. Give 'em a bit of time and they'll get tired of the place and move on.'

'Maybe,' Coulter said, 'but I don't think so. The varmint who shot my dog was askin' specially for Lodesville and it seems like he was arrangin' to meet this *hombre* Reber.'

June considered his comments. 'I don't think so either,' she replied. 'So I bin doin' some thinkin' and the only thing I can come up with is the Green Gulch Stage and Express Company.'

'The Green Gulch Stage and Express? What's that?'

'Previously known as the Lodesville and Western Direct. You might have come across it.'

'You mean those celerity wagons that come up to the hills deliverin' mail to the prospectors?'

'Yeah. Those wagons belonged to the Lodesville and Western Direct. They used 'em to take passengers up to Lone Creek and sometimes deliver mail and supplies beyond. It was only a small operation. I doubt whether they ever made any money out of it. Well, just recently, the Lodesville and Western got took over by some new operator. Changed its name, brought in some Concords, set up a few waystations between here and Penitence.'

'That's a long ways. Seems like it would need to carry a lot of passengers to make it pay.'

'I've heard Penitence is the up and coming place and there's talk about plans to extend the line clear through to California. Once that happens there'll be plenty of custom.'

Coulter's brow was lined with thought. 'Somethin' like that is goin' to take a lot of money to set up,' he mused. 'Banks is kinda scarce round these parts. Could be there's a hoard of ready loot on hand somewhere. Maybe in cash, maybe in gold or silver. Could be that Reber and the rest of these varmints got wind of it and figured to muscle in.' He turned to June. 'Have you any idea who is behind the stage company?'

'Used to be a man called Lorne Harrison. That was in the days when it was the Lodesville and Western. Seems like he sold out but I don't know who to.'

'Maybe we should look out this Harrison and see if we can find out anything further. Does he still live around these parts?'

'Sure. He's bought himself a little spread about twenty miles out of town. Calls it the Block H.'

Bragg had finished his meal and now spoke up. 'Better make it soon,' he said. 'Those gunslick varmints might be thinkin' the same thing.'

'You're right,' Coulter replied. 'And remember, the marshal will be lookin' out for us now. Let's get to the Block H before a posse's on our heels.'

They knew they were on Block H range when they began to see stray cattle. It was well into roundup time and only those cows that were still holding out in the draws and coulees remained to be brought in. As they approached the ranch they could see the cattle in the corrals waiting to be trail branded. Riding into the yard, they fastened their horses to a hitch rack as the door to the ranch house opened and a man appeared on the porch. He was small and thin with greying hair. Seeing June Campbell, he came down the steps.

'Well, hello,' he said. 'Didn't expect to see you out this far.'

'Hello, Lorne,' she replied. 'How's things with the ranchin'?'

A smile spread across his drawn features. 'It's hard work,' he said, 'but it sure beats sittin' in an office.'

'Let me introduce a couple o' friends o' mine.

Lorne Harrison, this is Rhett Coulter and Denver Bragg.'

The rancher gave Bragg a slightly hesitant look but a glance at Coulter seemed to reassure him.

'Nice to meet you, gents,' he said. 'Come on in. There's coffee on the boil.' Turning on his heels, he preceded them into the ranch house. It was small and neat, but something about it betrayed the lack of a woman's touch.

'Take a seat. Be right with you,' he said.

He went through to the kitchen and soon returned with a tray on which were four mugs and a pot of steaming coffee. He poured and then took a spare seat.

'Guess you must be wonderin' what we're doin' here,' June began.

'It's unexpected,' he said, 'but it's always a real pleasure to see you. How's the café doin'?' He turned to the others. 'Best damn cook in the county,' he said.

'Gotta agree with you there,' Coulter replied.

'Café's fine,' June answered. 'My cousin is lookin' after it for a few days.'

Harrison looked slightly uncomfortable.

'Sorry about Rance,' he said. 'I heard somethin' about what happened.'

Coulter looked at June. She seemed to have coloured slightly. A thought suddenly struck him. Had there been something between June and Rance Germain?

'He was a good man,' she replied.

There was a pause.

'In a way, what happened to Rance is why we're here.'

Harrison took a long sup of coffee. 'Yeah?' he replied. 'How do you mean?'

June looked across to Coulter. 'Guess you'd best answer that,' she replied.

Coulter nodded. He thought for a moment about where to begin before deciding to start right back with the dog. When he had finished Harrison got to his feet and went to a cabinet from which he produced a bottle and some glasses.

'I guess we could all use somethin' a little stronger,' he said. He poured drinks for them all. Then he turned to Coulter. 'So you reckon this man Reber is after takin' over the stage line?'

'He already seems to have taken over the town. Seems to me like you could be in some trouble as well.'

'How do you mean?'

'How many men have you got? You don't need to answer that. Thing is, if those gunslicks take it into their heads to target the Block H, you could be in a lot of trouble. You got cattle ready for a trail-drive. They might take it into their heads to take over the herd.'

'All this is speculation,' Harrison replied.

'Rance got killed,' June retorted. 'There's a gang

of gunslicks beatin' up the town right now. That ain't speculation.'

'They shot my dog,' Coulter added. 'That ain't speculation either.'

Harrison stroked his chin. 'Nope,' he said. 'It ain't speculation. I bin losin' some cows and the boys have noticed some hardcases hangin' around. Seems like too much of a coincidence that these varmints have appeared just about the same time as the Green Gulch Stage and Express is set to take off.' He leaned over and topped up their drinks.

'I sold the old Lodesville and Western to a man named Roberts. I never actually met him. He's based somewhere out St Louis way. I dealt with his agent. Name of Jed Owen. He's organizin' things from Green Gulch. I could give you an introduction if you thought it was goin' to help.'

'That's good,' Coulter said. 'We're kinda workin' in the dark, but that seems as good a place to start as any.'

Harrison grinned. 'And from what you've told me, I reckon you could all do with somewhere to hide out for a while. You're welcome to stay here, at least until things simmer down a bit.'

Coulter looked towards the others.

'It's sure nice of you to offer,' he said, 'but we wouldn't want to get you into any trouble.'

'If what you've said is right, looks like I'm already in it,' Harrison laughed.

He turned to the woman. 'Funny how things turn out. I sure never figured you as an outlaw, June,' he quipped. 'Look, why not stay? I'd be glad of a bit of company.'

Coulter thought about it. In a lot of ways it made sense. Besides, if the Block H was in any danger, it wouldn't hurt to have a couple more hands.

'I tell you what,' he said. 'We will stick around, but only if we can help out about the place. Reckon a couple of hands might come in useful right about this time.'

'You're right there. I could use some assistance with the rest of the roundup and the brandin'. You boys have any experience of ranch work?'

'Sure have. Just tell us what you need doin' and we'll do it.'

'And you can leave the cookin' to me,' June intervened.

'That clinches it,' Harrison said.

'Just so long as you know what you're gettin' into,' Coulter said. 'There's no reason to expect a posse comin' out this way, but we've still got the law to contend with.'

'Gun law,' Harrison replied. 'And that's somethin' nobody can afford to ignore.'

Despite Harrison's offer of rooms at the ranch, Coulter and Bragg took up residence in the bunkhouse where they were introduced to the foreman, a tough-looking cowboy with skin like tanned leather who went by the name of Logan. Nobody seemed to know his first name. He assigned them a role next morning fixing some fences. They hadn't been there long when they saw riders in the distance. Several times during the course of the day the same thing happened. When they got back later they informed Logan about it.

'Been a lot of comin' and goin',' he said. 'I don't like it. I guess it don't matter too much just so long as they keep away from Block H land. Just keep an eye out for anythin' that looks like rustlin'.'

That evening Coulter suggested that he might take a ride to Green Gulch the next day to have a word with the agent, Jed Owen.

'Where do I find him?' he asked Harrison.

'He's got an office above the general store. Tell you what, I'll come with you. It might make gettin' to see him a bit easier.'

'Want me to come too?' Bragg asked.

'No, better stay behind. Keep an eye on June. Watch out in case that posse comes by.'

Next morning Coulter and Harrison set off for Green Gulch. On the way they passed one of the new waystations which had been set up for the stagecoach company. At present it consisted only of the building and a corral. They were surprised to see a couple of horses in the corral.

'Guess Owen has already moved in a manager,' Harrison commented.

Apart from the horses, the station had a deserted look. They rode on until they arrived at Green Gulch which lay in a valley between two small hills. The place had a prosperous look about it. The main street was busy and they drew to a halt outside the general store. It was on a corner and Harrison led Coulter to a stairway at the back which led to Owen's office on the floor above. Arriving outside an unmarked door, Harrison knocked hard. There was no reply. He tried once more with the same result.

'Could be out of town on company business,' Harrison commented. 'I suggest we have something to eat and come back later.'

'Where's Owen stayin'?' Coulter asked.

'As far as I know, he's at the Alhambra hotel.'

'Let's try it. We can eat there anyway.'

They went back down the stairs and made their way along the street to the hotel. Entering the foyer, Harrison moved to the reception desk.

'We've come to see Mr Owen,' he said to the clerk. 'Which room would he be in?'

The clerk looked at them suspiciously. Harrison produced a couple of dollar bills.

Turning to the register, the clerk replied, 'Number nine. Second floor. I think I saw him go up about an hour ago.'

They started up the stairs. Coming to number nine, Harrison knocked on the door. There was no reply.

'Like I said, maybe he's out of town.'

'The clerk said he came up about an hour ago.'

'Yeah, I was forgettin'.'

Harrison knocked once more. There was still no answer. Just at that moment the desk clerk appeared at the top of the stairs.

'I've got a key,' he said. 'If you like, I could check.'

'Yeah, go ahead and open the door.'

The clerk stepped forward and placed the key in the lock. There was a click and the door opened but only slightly. The clerk pushed at it and it opened another fraction.

'Stand back,' Coulter snapped. Raising his leg, he kicked the door hard. It moved but not completely. He kicked it again and this time it opened enough for them to be able to squeeze through. Jammed against the door was a chair and lying on the floor in front of it a figure was sprawled. Coulter went down on one knee.

'He's hurt pretty bad,' he said. 'But he's still alive.'

The desk clerk looked bemused.

'Go and get a doctor,' Harrison ordered.

The clerk turned and went back through the door.

'Make it quick!' Coulter called.

They could hear feet clattering down the stairs. Harrison looked around the room. A door leading to a balcony was open and a curtain fluttered in the wind. Drawing his gun, he moved to the opening and stepped out. There were footprints and down below there were marks in the dust.

'Looks like whoever did this to Owen either got in or left via the balcony,' he said.

'That would account for the fact that the desk clerk never mentioned anything. Presumably he would have said if he'd noticed a stranger comin' up or down the stairs.'

Harrison joined Coulter. The injured man had been pistol whipped and there was an ugly wound across the top of his skull.

'What do you think they were after?' Harrison said.

'Information,' Coulter replied.

'Information about what?'

Coulter shrugged. 'Maybe about money. I figure there's a lot of it about somewhere. Maybe about the stagecoach operation.'

'Whatever it was, it seems to confirm your ideas,' Harrison said. 'It sure looks like Reber and his gang are out to sabotage the Green Gulch Stage and Express.'

'Or maybe take it over. Along with Lodesville.'

'And my ranch,' Harrison added.

Before long the doctor arrived and shortly after that the injured man groaned and opened his eyes.

'What happened?' he managed to say.

'Take care of him, Doc,' Coulter said. 'If you need us, we'll be downstairs in the dining-room.'

They were eating their meal when the marshal appeared.

'What do you boys know about this?' he said, drawing up a chair at their table.

Coulter shifted uneasily in his seat. Was there a chance that the marshal had already been informed that he was on the run? Harrison quickly explained what they were doing in Green Gulch, emphasizing Owen's role in the sale of the stagecoach company. If he had any suspicions the marshal did not show them. Getting to his feet, he raised his hat and made to move.

'How is Mr Owen?' Harrison enquired.

'He'll be OK. The doc has made him comfortable.'

'OK if we stop by before we leave town?'

The marshal shrugged. 'Can't see any reason why not,' he said.

When he had gone and they had finished their meal, Harrison and Coulter returned to room nine. They found Owen lying propped up on a pile of pillows with a bandage wrapped round his head. He looked grey and worn but he perked up a little when they entered.

'I gather I have you two to thank for finding me,' he said.

They seated themselves by his bedside.

'I know you,' he said to Harrison. 'You were the former owner of the Lodesville and Western.'

'That's right.'

Owen looked puzzled. 'So was you findin' me just

a coincidence, or is there more to it?'

Harrison told him something of their concerns.

'Looks like you might be right,' Owen commented, when he had finished.

'Have you any idea who attacked you?' Coulter asked.

Forgetting his injuries, Owen shook his head and winced with the pain.

'Nope. I came back to the hotel after doin' some work at the office. Whoever it was must have been waitin' for me. I don't remember nothin' about it.'

'You didn't see him?'

'No. It just come at me out of the blue.'

'He didn't ask you any questions?'

'Nope. Like I say, one minute I was walkin' through the door, the next I was seein' stars.'

Harrison turned to Coulter. 'Looks like you disturbed him while he was in here. I guess he didn't expect you to come back when you did. In which case, have you any idea what he might have been lookin' for?'

Owen's face was creased with pain and the effort of conversation. Finally he shook his head a mere fraction.

'I can't seem to think straight,' he said.

'Never mind. You need to rest up. We'll be leavin' town later but we'll stop by to see you again before we go.'

They got up and had already started for the door

when Owen suddenly called them back.

'I think I know what it might have been they were after,' he said. He pointed to a bureau standing in one corner of the room. 'Look in the right-hand drawer,' he said.

Harrison opened the drawer. It was empty.

'Try the others,' the man said.

Harrison did so but they were empty too.

'Hell,' Owen said. 'Whoever it was must have took it.'

Coulter stepped to his side. 'Taken what?' he said.

'The letter. From St Louis.' He stopped, pain written across his features. Making an effort he started to speak again.

'It was from Norman Roberts in St Louis. Sayin' he was comin' to Green Gulch and he's bringin' a whole parcel of bullion with him.'

Coulter and Harrison exchanged glances.

'It's the sort of thing he might do,' Owen continued. 'He's decided now to take personal charge of things.'

'Did he say when he's comin'?' Coulter asked.

'Yeah. He'll be on the noon stage from Owlcreek Crossing on the twenty third. It's scheduled to be the first on the new route.'

'That's two days' time,' Harrison said.

Coulter turned back to the invalid. 'Thanks for the information,' he said. 'It could be crucial.'

'What do you folks intend doin'?'

'We ain't too sure, but I reckon we'd best meet up with Mr Roberts before he gets on that stage.'

'Or be on it with him,' Coulter said.

When they got back to the Block H, Coulter and Harrison told Bragg and June what they had learned.

'What's the plan?' Bragg asked.

'I aim to be on the stage,' Coulter replied.

'That stage will be comin' right through Lodesville *en route* to Green Gulch. You could be ridin' straight into trouble.'

'I'll be wearin' a disguise,' Coulter joked. 'Besides, it was Bragg they put in the slammer. I'm not sure how much they know about me.'

'If Reber attacks that stage, you'll be one against how many?' June put in.

'There'll be someone ridin' shotgun. I figure the odds won't be so bad.'

'Why not just warn Roberts off?'

'For one thing, I want to put our theories to the test. For all we know for sure, we could still be barkin' up the wrong tree.'

'Why don't me and some of the boys cover the route?' Harrison said. 'Bragg could come along too. He wouldn't be recognized.'

'Yeah, why not? Sounds like a good plan to me. But keep out of sight. Don't let Reber and his gang know you're there.'

The next day Coulter rode to Owlcreek Crossing. It lay on the other side of Lodesville to Green Gulch and a spur line ran to it from the railroad. Reserving himself a seat on the next day's stage, Coulter booked in to an hotel for the night.

'Have you got a booking name of Roberts?' he asked the desk clerk.

The man looked in the register. 'Nope,' he replied. 'Were you expectin' somebody?'

Coulter hadn't anticipated a positive reply. It was worth a try, but it was much more likely that Roberts would be coming in on the morning train. It occurred to Coulter to go back and ask a similar question at the stagecoach depot but then he reflected that there wasn't much point. Roberts would be there or he wouldn't. Besides, if he asked questions he might arouse suspicion. He had a good description of the man from Owen – large and florid and with distinctive side whiskers. It was unlikely that he would mistake him.

The next day he was at the stage depot early. A little crowd had gathered and hung across the street was a banner saying:

Green Gulch Stage and Express. Speed, Comfort and Elegance.

Standing outside the depot was a new-looking stage-coach, one of the bigger Concord types that June had mentioned. Coulter stood back to admire it. The body of the coach was green and the chassis and wheels a brilliant yellow. Coming up close, he glanced through the large window. The interior was plush lined and fitted with three upholstered bench seats and small candle lamps. He reckoned there was room inside for up to a dozen passengers. A team of six horses was being fitted to the traces.

'Sure looks perty,' someone said at his elbow.

He glanced round to see an elderly man wearing a smart black suit.

'You takin' a ride?' Coulter asked.

'Sure am. Wouldn't have missed it. Name's Sparrow, Henry P. Sparrow.'

'Nice to meet you. Rhett Coulter.'

They began to observe some of the other likely passengers – a couple in their forties with a young boy, an eager looking man with the appearance of a lawyer and another man carrying what looked like a bag of samples. There was no sign of anyone resembling the description of Norman Roberts. The clerk of the depot was now acting in the role of porter and stacking baggage on top of the stage and in the front and rear boots. The horses were ready. The clock inside the depot ticked its way steadily towards the noon hour. Coulter was beginning to think that Owen must have got it wrong when suddenly the braying notes of a trumpet burst upon the air playing a rendition of 'Yankee Doodle'. The next moment the door of the depot flung open and a big burly man who unmistakably fitted Norman Roberts's description appeared. The crowd fell into silence as the last notes of the trumpet died away. Advancing, Roberts began to address the crowd.

'Ladies and gentlemen, today is an auspicious day in the history not only of our region but of the entire West. Today the country has been opened to advancement and settlement by the creation of the Green Gulch Stage and Express Company. Today you can travel in a luxury never experienced before.'

The crowd broke into cheering. Roberts held up his hand and continued in a similar vein, continuing to put an emphasis on the word *today*. Coulter's eyes travelled past the group at the depot and swept the street to right and left. There was nothing to arouse suspicion. One way was the town, the other way the road led past the outlying stores and houses till it passed on a low trestle bridge across Owl Creek which gave the place its name.

'Speed, comfort and elegance,' the voice of Roberts continued. 'Yes, that's our aim, our vision, and our pledge. From today, from this day forward, travel will never be the same again. Ladies and gentlemen, the moment has come, the time has arrived. Today a new chapter opens. All aboard for the first historic journey of what is destined to become one of the legends of the West. I give you the Green Gulch Stage and Express.'

Another shout went up. Someone yelled 'Three cheers!' and there was further commotion as Roberts held the stage door open for the first passengers to enter. Coulter took his seat last, sitting alongside the old timer who had introduced himself as Sparrow. Finally Roberts himself took his seat, slamming the heavy door behind him. He smiled at the others inside and then knocked on the roof.

There was a sound of feet shuffling from up above and then the crack of a whip. Slowly the stage edged forward, moving through the main street of town. A number of people were lining the boardwalks and they waved and cheered as the stage rolled along. The buildings passed by, the people dwindled in number and finally they were on the trail outside of town, picking up speed as they went. Roberts smiled around at everyone once more and then settled into a corner seat opposite Coulter. He did not carry any baggage with him. If there was any bullion on board, it must have been stashed with the rest of the baggage. Coulter had been observing Roberts for any signs of tension such as carrying a lot of money might invoke but he seemed completely natural and relaxed. There was absolutely no trace of concern. Coulter sat back and began to enjoy the ride. The coach was certainly more comfortable than anything comparable that he had ridden in before. Soon the rest of the people began to unwind. The couple with the child asked if anyone minded the window being open a little. Nobody objected and the young man with the bag of samples, now stored in the forward boot, adjusted the canvas curtain and did the honours. The oldster in the black suit, who had introduced himself as Henry P. Sparrow, unloosed his tie a little and made a comment about the armrest which was fitted into the base of the window.

'Latest design, latest design,' Roberts piped up. 'Nothing but the best.'

Coulter wondered whether the others knew that he was the boss of the operation. From the speech-making he guessed that they knew he was somebody important.

'Over a thousand dollars each coach,' Roberts continued, 'and that's without the extras.'

Coulter turned his attention to the scene outside, which was partly obscured by the curtain. Away off he could see the line of the hills where he and Bragg had been prospecting and just coming down off them a herd of wild horses.

'Mustangs,' Roberts commented. 'When they're tamed down they make for a mighty fine team.'

Coulter watched the mustangs for a little distance until they disappeared below a dip in the ground.

'Got me a steady supply,' Roberts added. 'It's good business.'

After leaving Lodesville, the next stop, the coach would follow a curve in the trail that would take them past a spur of the hills. Thinking of Lodesville put Coulter on the alert. If the marshal or anyone else recognized him, he could be in trouble. He hoped that the stage would not stay long and that there would be no further demonstrations of civic pride. Eventually the stagecoach began to pass through familiar territory. They would soon be approaching Lodesville. At a spot where a trail leading to the hills met the main trail they were following, he looked out and saw in the distance the shape of one of the smaller, lighter coaches making its way towards the diggings. He glanced across at Roberts who had seen it too and wore a smile across his countenance. He had evidently bought into a profitable business with plenty of scope for expansion.

Eventually the stagecoach clattered into Lodesville. There were several people waiting outside the depot but there was none of the fanfare there had been at Owlcreek Crossing. Although he knew there wasn't really much chance that he might be recognized, Coulter made himself inconspicuous by drawing further into the corner and pulling his hat lower over his eyes. The door on the opposite side opened and three more people climbed in, a middle-aged woman and a couple of men dressed in range gear. Without wasting too much time the driver climbed back on his seat beside the guard and they were on their way again. Coulter had made a point of sizing up the guard. He was a man of about forty. He looked capable and as if he knew how to handle the Winchester Model 1866 he carried.

Coulter sat up and looked out of the window

again. Dust from the horses' hoofs had stained the glass. They were going at a good pace. The ride was comparatively smooth but still the coach lurched from time to time and there were creaks and groans as the framework adjusted to the contours of the trail. Coulter was truly alert now because if there was to be any sort of incident it would have to be before they reached Green Gulch where, according to Owen, Roberts intended to disembark. The coach swayed. They had reached the big bend in the trail where the spur of the hills stretched down to meet the plains. Suddenly Coulter knew that the attack, if it was to happen, would happen when they rounded that bend. The driver's vision would be more limited and there would be cover for any riders. He had an urge to warn the others but he knew it wouldn't do any good. The only thing he could do was to be ready and hope that Harrison and Bragg were on hand if things got rough.

The coach was taking the big bend. Coulter leaned forward and at the same moment there was a loud report followed by a number of other shots. The coach began to lurch forward with increased speed. The woman who had got into the carriage at Lodesville let out an involuntary gasp and, as the coach gathered speed, the young boy was flung to the floor. The sounds of shooting from outside were unmistakable.

'Everybody get down!' Coulter yelled.

'What's happening?' the middle-aged woman screamed.

Coulter threw down the window and leaned out. Coming down from the hills was a group of riders coming at the coach at a tangent and firing their guns as they did so. There was a loud booming crash from up above as the guard discharged his rifle. Coulter had his guns out and was firing, aware that the young drummer had drawn a gun and was firing out of the other window. That could only mean one thing: they were being attacked from that side as well. The horses were plunging forward now at breakneck speed and the coach had begun to sway noticeably from side to side. Someone screamed and then the next instant the coach reared up on two wheels, lurched along for a few more yards in that crazy position and then went over on its side. Everything was confusion. The coach dragged along the ground for several yards till the horses, frenzied by the noise of gunfire and tangled up in their traces, were dragged over by the weight of the coach. Plunging and snorting, they struggled madly to regain their feet.

Coulter managed to get to the door as Roberts pushed it open. The two of them scrambled out on to the side of the overturned coach. Coulter didn't have time to worry about what had happened to the others. The driver had jumped to one side and the guard had been thrown headlong from his seat on top of the coach. He had landed a short distance away, but was still firing at the oncoming gunslicks. Coulter slid down from the coach and, taking cover, continued to blaze away at the attackers. They were almost upon them now, approaching from two sides. The trail was littered with baggage and despite the turmoil, Coulter saw a group of the attackers pick something up – it looked like a metal box – and, carrying it to a waiting horse, start riding away.

'Stop them!' a voice shouted.

Coulter turned. The voice was that of Roberts. Beside himself, he staggered to his feet and waving his arms wildly, started in pursuit of the fast disappearing riders. A bullet caught him and spun him round. He flung up his arms and fell head first to the ground. A bullet tore into the dust beside Coulter and then he felt something graze his cheek. Blood was flowing. He looked up as a rider approached with a rifle held at arm's length. Coulter turned and raised his Colt, but before he could fire the rider went hurtling from his horse and hit the ground in a cloud of dust. Coulter glanced behind him. Sparrow was there with a smoking gun in his hand.

The conflict began to die down as the bushwhackers rode away from the scene. Coulter got to his feet and continued firing at the retreating gunmen but suddenly became aware that he was the only one doing so. He looked to his left where the guard had been flung but there was no movement from him.

He stopped and looked about him. The last of the riders was disappearing in the distance and in place of the crackle of gunfire there was an eerie silence broken only by someone sobbing and a series of low moans from the direction of the coach. Hearing footsteps behind him, Coulter turned, his gun at the ready, but it was only Sparrow. The stagecoach driver had struggled to his feet and now came limping up.

'Help me get the rest of them out of the coach,' Coulter said.

They turned back. Most of the passengers had managed to struggle free with the help of the able-bodied men, but the middle-aged lady and the mother of the young boy were still trapped inside together with the man who had returned fire. Coulter climbed back into the coach and with the driver assisting from above, succeeded in extricating the two women from the wreckage, but when he got to the man it was clear that he was dead. The window of the coach had shattered and his head had been dragged along the ground. There wasn't much left to recognize him by. Coulter felt his gorge rise and quickly turned away. Pulling himself up, he climbed back to the side of the coach and then dropped to the ground.

A few of the passengers had had the presence of mind to see to the horses. Two of them had been shot dead and a third was in a bad way with its injuries. It lay in a pitiful state till Coulter drew his gun and put it out of its misery. He moved to where the guard lay. He was dead, shot several times through the chest. Coulter was about to look and see what had happened to Roberts when the man appeared, staggering towards them. A shot had grazed his arm but it was only a minor injury. The women were sobbing and the boy was crying. One of the other men had been hit in the shoulder. The rest of them were badly shaken and in distress. Roberts was in a frantic state but it wasn't clear whether it was because of his wounded arm or because the gunmen had made off with his money. To Coulter it seemed there was something almost histrionic about it. But through all the confusion and dismay one thought kept drumming through Coulter's head: what had happened to Bragg and Harrison? What had gone wrong with the plans they had laid? If they had arrived as expected they could have held off the gunmen. As it was Coulter felt a deep sense of frustration and shame. He had let these people down. He should have done a lot better. Whoever Reber was, he had won again.

CHAPTER THREE

It wasn't too far to Green Gulch. There was nothing to be done other than to get back into the stagecoach and reach the town. The problem was righting the vehicle but after strenuous efforts on everyone's part and the pulling power of the remaining horses, they succeeded in doing so. When they had completed the task the middle-aged lady, one of the few who still managed to remain in full control of themselves, asked what was to be done about the dead.

'Perhaps we'd best leave 'em,' Roberts said. 'The undertaker can come out from Green Gulch.'

There was some discussion. The driver was reluctant to leave the guard and in the end he won the day and the bodies were loaded into the rear boot. It was a gruesome business. When that task was accomplished the driver climbed back on to the box, cracked his whip, and the stage moved forward slowly. It was a sorry scene inside. Such measures as could be managed had been taken to attend the wounds of the injured but it seemed a long and agonizing journey before the town came into view. Coulter was thinking hard. He wanted to avoid the scenes that would take place at the stage depot. Although it was a slim chance that he would be recognized he needed to avoid that possibility. At the same time he was puzzled about Bragg and Harrison. They had made their plans; it was obvious that something must have happened to them to prevent them coming to the stage's assistance. Had the gunslicks come upon them? The more he thought about it the more likely it seemed. He came to a decision. As soon as the stage reached town he would slip away, get quickly to the livery stable and acquire a horse. He would ride up into the spur of the hills to see if he could find any trace of his comrades.

There were a number of people gathered at the depot and there seemed to be an air of agitation about the place, almost as if word had already got out about what had happened to the stage. Even before the stage had come to a halt Coulter had opened the door and jumped to the ground.

'Get the doctor,' he said. 'There's been a hold up.'

He moved round towards the door of the depot as if seeking the desk clerk, but turning immediately to his left, began to move away quickly. He was assisted in his endeavours to remain unnoticed by the hullabaloo which had broken out behind him. Ducking down an alley he came to the rear entrance to the stables. There were some horses in a corral at the back and Coulter called for the ostler to saddle him one. The ostler looked dubiously at Coulter's somewhat dishevelled state but the sight of money soon persuaded him to get on with business without asking questions. Coulter stepped into the leather and with a nod at the ostler rode the horse out the back. Keeping to the side streets he was soon out of town and heading back by a circuitous route which would keep him out of the way of the scenes that were taking place at the stagecoach depot. Answering to his firm but gentle touch, the horse broke into a trot and then a gallop as Coulter guided it towards the foothills. As he climbed towards higher ground the trail the stage had come along was below him and soon he could see the remains of the horses. The riders had come down from this point and he began to scan the ground for any tell-tale signs of what might have happened to Bragg and Harrison. It was easy enough to see where the gunslicks had been. They had left a trail a child could have followed. It led back along a low ridge which led eventually up into the hills but after a time it branched away from the ridge in the direction of a valley which Coulter calculated would eventually lead him in the direction of the Block H. It was late in the day and the sun was fast sinking below the western horizon but Coulter continued to ride. He had expected the trail to veer off, maybe back in the direction of Green Gulch, but it continued on towards the Block H. Coulter began to feel a new fear. Unless the trail diverged soon, the signs were that Reber and his men had come from the ranch itself. What might he find when he got there?

Night brought with it a gusting wind and a spatter of rain. It was harder to make out the gunslicks' traces but it didn't matter. Coulter was simply aiming now for the Block H. Towards midnight he stopped at a waterhole for the horse to rest and drink and then he was on his way again. It couldn't be far now. The rain had almost stopped. Pulling his hat down low he pushed the horse as hard as it would safely go; speed had become relevant but he didn't want to damage the beast. Although he could discern little of the surrounding country he had a feeling that he was close to the ranch. He felt uneasy. The horse's ears were pricked and it too seemed to sense that something was wrong. Then he noticed the smell. It was an acrid, gritty odour, as yet faint but growing stronger. He knew what it was: it was the smell of burning. When he topped a slight rise he had his first dim sight of the ranch house. It was little more than a still smouldering pile of ashes. Behind it the outhouses were also burnt out except for a corner of one of the barns. The corrals were trampled down and there was no sign of the cattle apart from the churned up ground where they had stampeded. In one corner of the corral stood an abandoned wagon.

Coulter spurred his horse and rode into the yard. As he dismounted a shot rang out, sending his horse rearing. Flinging himself to the ground he rolled into the shelter of a water trough. A second shot rang out, whining as it ricocheted from the metal of the trough. The shots had come from the direction of the barn. Coulter began to crawl towards some bushes and, as he did so, a third bullet tore up the dust not far from his leg. Getting instantly to his feet, he made a dash for cover. Another shot tore into the trees ahead of him but it was wildly off target. Reaching the shelter of the bushes, Coulter began to circle towards what was left of the barn, approaching it from the rear. Coming up behind one of the ruined corrals, he could see inside the shattered building. Someone was in there, crouched near the doorway. He raised his rifle and was about to squeeze the trigger when something about the partly concealed figure arrested his attention. Lowering the gun, he peered carefully. It wasn't a man after all. It was a woman and that could only mean it was June. Cupping his hand to his mouth, Coulter called to her.

'Don't shoot. It's me, Coulter!'

Taken by surprise she quickly turned her head, raising her rifle as she did so.

'It's Coulter!' he shouted again. 'Look, I'm behind the corral. I'm going to stand up and throw my rifle to one side.'

She was obviously jumpy and he realized he would be taking a risk. Still he rose to his feet, holding the rifle at arm's length before throwing it away from him. He was acutely conscious of the rifle pointed at his chest and for a brief moment everything seemed to stand suspended. Then the tension was broken.

'Coulter!' she shouted. 'I thought you were one of the outlaws!'

In a few seconds he had rushed forward and she was in his arms and sobbing with relief. He held her close and let the tension ebb out of her before finally holding her away from him.

'What happened?' he said. 'Where's Bragg?'

She shook her head and seemed unable to speak.

'Where is Bragg?' he repeated.

She looked at him with open, tear-stained eyes.

'I think Bragg's dead,' she said.

Coulter released his hold of her and moved towards the barn door. June seemed to get a grip of herself and caught his arm.

'Back there,' she said and began to move towards the barn. Coulter followed her outside and round to the opposite side. Lying in the grass were a number of corpses Coulter had not seen from his previous perspective and a short distance off the body of Bragg. Coulter rushed over and knelt down. It was riddled with bullets and it seemed he must be dead, but when Coulter put his ear to Bragg's mouth he though he could hear a faint breathing.

'Wait here,' he said to June.

He rushed off and was quickly back with a canteen of water and some medicines from his war bag. Lifting the wounded man's head as gently as he could, he poured water between his swollen lips.

'Guess he could do with something a little stronger.'

This time he tipped some whiskey down Bragg's throat and, after a few moments the man's eyelids flickered and opened. A feeble attempt at a grin spread across his features and he attempted to speak but managed only an indistinct mutter.

'Don't leave us,' Coulter said.

With June's assistance he succeeded in cleaning and bandaging the worst of Bragg's injuries. Obviously the outlaws had ridden away leaving him for dead but the man was strong and Coulter reckoned he might have a chance of survival if he could get some proper treatment.

'We need to get him to a doc,' he said.

'The wagon,' June replied.

In an instant Coulter was on his feet and running to his horse. It was no easy matter to harness the horse to the wagon, but with a bit of improvisation Coulter, with June's assistance, managed to do it. Between them they lifted the wounded man and placed him as carefully as they could in the wagon.

'It's not too far back to Lodesville. I'll drive if you

get in and keep an eye on him.'

'What about the marshal?' June asked.

'I'll have to take my chance,' he replied.

The horse took the strain and slowly the wagon began to roll forward. It would be a slow journey but the horse, a palomino, was big and strong and Coulter had no doubts but that they would eventually get to town. As they moved he told June what had happened to the stagecoach and she told him the whole story of events at the Block H. After he had left for Green Gulch a gang of riders had approached the ranch house. Whether by accident or design they had chosen the right moment. Harrison was away rounding up some stray cattle and only one man had been left behind along with Bragg. Thinking it was the posse come to arrest him, Bragg had at first hidden in the house but it soon became apparent it wasn't a posse. As they approached and the remaining ranch-hand had gone out to meet them, they had opened fire, killing him instantly. June had retreated to the barn while Bragg had succeeded in putting up a fight and holding the outlaws at bay till they started hurling firebrands which set the ranch house on fire. Under Bragg's directions she had taken shelter in the trees. Bragg had continued to fight but he hadn't a chance. They finally cornered him in the barn. Bursting out, he had put up what had seemed to be his last stand.

'Where's Harrison now?' Coulter asked.

'I don't know. The outlaws ran off most of the cattle. My guess is that he and Logan are off tracking them, not realizing yet what's happened here.'

As they lurched out of the yard Coulter and June took a last look about them. There were charred remains among the ashes and they could also see a couple of other bodies in the grass outside. There was little that could be salvaged from the burnt-out ranch house. Harrison would have to start all over again.

It was evening. Coulter and June were sitting in the little room behind the eating house. June's cousin had locked the place for the day and for the time being they were safe from outside interference. Bragg lay in a room upstairs. The doctor had spent some time cutting out bullets from his side, his upper leg and his shoulder but he seemed confident that Bragg would pull through.

'What happened?' the doctor asked.

'Shootout with some rustlin' *hombres,*' Coulter said, without going into any details. They were making out that Bragg had been riding for one of the spreads. Whether the doctor believed them or not, he was a man of the world and had been round long enough not to ask too many questions.

'Change the bandages regularly and make sure the wounds are kept clean,' he said. He turned to June. 'I don't need to tell you to keep his strength up with good food. Plenty of hot broth. I'll call back, see how he's doin'. It's really just a question of time.'

When he had gone, Coulter turned to June.

'Looks like he'll have to stay here. How do you feel about it?'

'I doubt that anyone got a good look at me that night,' she said. 'Or you, for that matter. It's Bragg himself the marshal knows.'

'Do you think the doc will keep his mouth shut?'

'I have no worry in that regard,' June said. 'He's an old friend of mine.' She paused for a moment. 'And of Rance Germain. If he doesn't know about the new marshal already, I figure it won't be long till he's feelin' about the same as we do.' She summoned up a smile. 'No, the real pity is I was just gettin' the hang of ridin' with you two. Now I'm back here again.'

Coulter returned her smile. 'Only till Bragg's able to mount a horse again,' he said.

She poured two mugs of coffee.

'What about you?' she asked.

Coulter took a long drink.

'Reckon I need to locate Harrison first of all,' he said. 'After that I ain't so sure. Find this man Reber. He seems to be the brains behind it all.'

'He can't have too many of those,' she said.

Coulter threw her a quizzical glance.

'Killin' your dog wasn't enough for him,' she said. 'Seems to me he's got a whole lot more to answer for now.'

'He wasn't the one did the shootin',' Coulter commented.

June got up and moved to the window, glancing out into the night, before turning back to Coulter.

'This man Reber,' she said. 'Are you sure he's the one you're after?'

'How do you mean?' Coulter said.

'Well, we're assumin' that the riders who approached Bragg at the diggings were part of his gang and makin' their way to meet him. But think back. What did Bragg say they said to him?'

'From what he told me, they asked him the way to Lodesville and said that they were lookin' for a man named Reber.'

'Yeah. You know what that suggests to me? That they didn't know who Reber was.'

Coulter was quiet, weighing up her words.

'Pity we can't ask Bragg just exactly what they said right now,' he commented.

'Think about it,' June replied. 'If they had arranged to meet Reber they wouldn't have been asking if Bragg knew who he was. To me it looks like they knew the name but not the man. They were askin' Bragg so that he could describe him to them, or even point him out.'

'So what's your guess about them?'

'My guess, and it may be way out of line, is that we've got two groups on our hands. Reber and the first came to Lodesville where they caused trouble and ended up shootin' Rance Germain. The second group is lookin' for Reber but they don't know exactly who he is.'

Coulter considered the matter.

'You could be right,' he concluded. 'If that is the case, which of them is responsible for what happened to the stagecoach and which for what happened at the Block H? And what's the connection between them? Does each know the other even exists?'

'We know it was Reber killed the marshal,' June said.

Coulter looked across at her. She had sat down again but had turned her face from him.

'June,' he said, 'I hope you don't mind me askin', but was there somethin' between you and Rance Germain?'

He thought he detected a slight movement of her shoulders before she turned to face him.

'Why do you ask that?' she said.

'Oh, I don't know. Just something in the way you've spoken about him. You seemed to get awful mad about the townsfolk not standin' up to the outlaws.'

She nodded. 'You're right,' she replied. 'Used to be somethin', a while ago. Pretty much ended between us before all this. I guess that's why I was so down on the townsfolk. Look at the doc. They ain't so bad really, I guess.'

'Sorry,' Coulter replied.

'No need to be sorry. Like I say, it was over between us.'

There was a pause. The silence lay heavy between them. Outside in the dark a nightjar began to call.

'I'd say that Reber is likely to be right here in town,' June continued eventually. 'After all, if we're right he's got the marshal behind him.'

'In which case his plan was probably to just walk right on in and take the place over. Meanwhile those varmints that shot my dog were lookin' for him. They knew about Lodesville so they probably were in on his plans. Maybe they were all in Reber's gang and they had a fallout.'

'You're forgettin' that we're assumin' now that those varmints didn't know who Reber was.'

'If Reber's plan was to take over the town and therefore by implication the stage company, there would be no sense in him attacking the stage. That must have been the other lot. By attacking the stage they would be attackin' Reber.'

June suddenly looked animated. 'And that would mean it was Reber attacked the ranch. Maybe he got word that we were hidin' out there. Maybe he persuaded the marshal to raise a posse and it was them burned down the ranch after all.'

'The posse, Reber's gang of owlhoots – what's the difference? Probably one and the same. Hell,' Coulter said, 'I think we're really gettin' somewhere with this.' He got to his feet and began to pace the floor.

'The coyotes that attacked the stage got away with Roberts's loot. They weren't expectin' any opposition. Maybe if I hadn't have been there they'd have killed Roberts as well. Reber will want that money.'

'Hold it there. In effect Reber's taken over the town. He must have known about the Green Gulch and Western. What if Reber and Roberts are in on this together?'

'Then how would the others have known about the loot?'

They both stopped, lost in thought.

'Should I make some fresh coffee?' June asked.

'Yeah. That would be nice.'

June went back into the kitchen. Coulter could hear her at the stove. Suddenly he slapped his hand across his thigh.

'I've got it,' he shouted.

June appeared in the doorway.

'Let's assume Reber and Roberts are in this together,' he continued. 'Then Roberts could have arranged the whole stage robbery as an elaborate hoax in order to get the money all to himself. In that case the varmints who attacked the stage would in fact have been acting on his orders. They were in Roberts's pay. In which case the fact that I was there only served to make matters worse. I thought I was actin' for the best but I had exactly the opposite effect.'

June ducked back into the kitchen and re-emerged with a fresh pot of coffee. She poured it out thick and strong.

'I think you could be right,' she said. 'I don't know. The whole thing seems a bit elaborate. But it makes sense. Apart from Roberts gettin' shot, that is.'

'That was an accident. It wasn't part of the plot but it worked out quite well. Made Roberts look even cleaner. Reber won't have any reason to suspect Roberts. Leastways not yet. He'll want that money back. Reckon I can leave Reber for the moment. We need to find where they've taken the money.'

'There's one easy way to find that out,' June said. 'At least, if we're right about this. And what's more, it'll be one sure fire way of finding out whether we're right or not.'

'What's that?' Coulter said.

'Just think. If Roberts planned the hold-up, he'll know where the money's been taken. Roberts is the key. Get on to Roberts, persuade him to tell you where the money's gone, and you'll find the owl-hoots.'

'I'll find the man who killed my dog,' Coulter added. 'In fact, if we're right, Roberts is indirectly responsible. But that still leaves the varmints who almost killed Bragg.'

'Not to mention what they did to the ranch. But then Reber is not such a problem. We know he's around town someplace. He can wait.'

Coulter's eyes met June's. She still looked flushed and excited. For a moment they held their gaze and then June looked down. Coulter suddenly felt awkward.

'Hey, better go up and check on Bragg,' he said.

He went up the stairs and crept into the bedroom where the big man had been laid. Bragg was breathing heavily and didn't look too good. Coulter bent over him and adjusted the covers which had been flung about. As he did so Bragg gave a big sigh and one eye flickered open.

'That you, Coulter?' he whispered in a hoarse voice.

'Sure is,' Coulter replied. 'How are you doin'?'

'Feel like hell, but I sure could use a drink.'

Bragg smiled. 'Takes more than a few bullets to put you down for long,' he replied. 'Whiskey do?'

'Make it a double,' Bragg said. 'In fact, you might leave the bottle.'

Coulter went down the stairs to the kitchen. By the time he returned with the whiskey Bragg was sound asleep.

For a man who had lost a lot of money and been shot into the bargain, Norman Roberts was in a remarkably good frame of mind. Standing at the bar of the Black Diamond saloon, his left hand bandaged, he was standing drinks to a number of regulars and others when Coulter came through the batwings.

Even before he was halfway across the floor Roberts spotted him and shouted for him to come over.

'Boys,' he said, 'let me introduce you to a friend of mine.' He turned to Coulter, 'I'm sorry,' he said, 'but just for the moment I can't recall your name.'

'Rhett Coulter,' Coulter responded.

'That's the man. Did a goldarned good job fightin' off those varmints that attacked the stage. Bartender, open another bottle. Here, the drinks are on me.'

Coulter poured himself a drink from the proffered bottle.

'Yes siree, I reckon the town could do with a few true men and honest citizens like Mr Coulter.' He stood with his back to the bar and looking Coulter up and down, continued, 'A toast, everyone. To my good friend and colleague, Mr Rhett Coulter.' There was a burst of laughter and then a few voices took up the refrain:

'Mr Rhett Coulter!'

Coulter smiled, nodded his head in acquiescence, and swallowed a slug of liquor. It burnt its way down his throat, but he knew exactly how much he could afford to down and stay alert. If Roberts was putting on a show, he was doing a good job of it. He sounded completely genuine but one look at some of his fellows at the bar did a lot to convince Coulter that he was right in his surmises after all. Among the usual types there was a good sprinkling of some ornery-looking varmints who looked like they could be very handy with a gun.

'You handled yourself pretty well,' Coulter said.

'It was nothin'. The Green Gulch Stage and Express don't stop for anything.'

'The show goes on,' Coulter commented.

'Exactly. The show goes on and the next stage will be leavin' right on time.' Roberts was certainly in an expansive mood. Suddenly he stopped and gave Coulter a searching look.

'Say,' he said, 'Mr Coulter, what would you say to the offer of a job? Are you doin' anythin' just at present?'

'Nope,' Coulter replied. 'Can't say as I'm fixed just at the moment. What sort of a job did you have in mind?'

'Why, shotgun guard of course. After the way you handled yourself out there, what else could it be? You'd be just the man for the job, just the sort of fella I'm lookin' for.'

Coulter was thinking fast. He had sought Roberts out at the saloon but he had no clear idea about how he was to get the information he wanted out of him. There could be a way, but what? If he took up this job offer he would be on the inside of Roberts's and Reber's operation. A chance would surely present itself of tracking the outlaws to their den.

'You ain't said nothin' about wages,' he said.

'Top dollar of course. And perks thrown in. I supply you with your rifle and ammunition. Got some place to stay?'

Again Coulter thought fast.

'Nowhere's special,' he said.

'There's room out at the first waystation if you want it,' Roberts continued. 'Bed and board, good money, extras thrown in. That seems a pretty good offer to me.'

'Sounds a pretty good offer to me as well.'

'Then you'll take the job?'

'Sure will. When do I report for duty?'

Roberts let out a hefty guffaw.

'Next stage leaves day after tomorrow. Be there at the depot at eight. If you like, take a ride over towards Green Gulch and take a look at your new lodgings in the meantime. Tell you what: the stage could pick you up there. You'll find the waystation without any trouble.'

Coulter took a last long swig of whiskey. The waystation offer would have clinched the deal even if he hadn't already accepted the job. This way he would avoid the possibility of running into the marshal either in town or at the depot.

'Then it's a deal,' he said. 'And thank you, Mr Roberts.'

'Call in at the gun store. Buy yourself whatever you'll need. Charge it to me.'

Coulter moved towards the batwings. Out of the corner of his eye he could see Roberts in discussion with one of the ornery-looking *hombres* standing next to him at the bar. Either Roberts, probably under the influence of drink, was being straight or he was being set up. Either way he would need to be on his guard.

Having explained the situation to June, next day Coulter rode out in the direction of Green Gulch. June had seemed unusually reluctant to let him go and as he rode, he could still hear her words ringing in his ears telling him to be careful. Strangely, he found that he was missing her too, although they had been together so little. It was a bright day. The bad weather had cleared and despite his concerns about Bragg he felt a surge of energy. He rode for most of the morning, allowing the horse to go at its own pace; towards the middle of the afternoon he saw the waystation ahead of him. It didn't amount to much, but it was obvious that it had been newly built. It was a long low building of adobe and the newly white-washed walls seemed almost to glint in the sun. There was a stable and a small corral at the back but at present it was empty of horses. Coulter rode into the yard and tethering the palomino to the hitch rail stepped up on to the porch. Standing there for a moment, he glanced around him before opening the door. The place was bare with just a long table and a few straight-backed wooden chairs, but it had a solid plank floor. At the back there was a door leading to another room. Stepping across, Coulter looked inside. There was a bunk bed and a chest of drawers. A small window looked out on the corral with some trees beyond it.

'Not so bad,' Coulter said to himself.

He wondered when whoever was taking it over would be arriving. There didn't seem much point in the stage stopping at this juncture. There was nothing to stop for. It would be simpler just to carry on, perhaps stop at Green Gulch. He supposed it would be different when the stageline really got going. Perhaps the idea was to miss out Green Gulch and avoid a bit of a detour. Still, why should he concern himself? He had a place for as long as he might need it. Walking back outside he took the things he would need and carried them inside before leading the horse to the corral. Then he set about making himself something to eat. By the time he had finished the afternoon was fast drawing towards evening. He stood outside on the porch with a mug of coffee in his hands. The sun was low on the horizon and a breeze had sprung up. Behind the buildings the leaves of the trees rattled softly. Suddenly he tensed. He thought he heard something else, he couldn't be certain what. Placing the mug on a step of the porch, he listened intently. When he was finally convinced that he must have been mistaken he bent down to pick up the mug. There it was again, a very faint shuffling sound. He still couldn't quite place what it was, but it was something that didn't quite fit in with the soughing of the breeze, the whispering of the leaves. Off in the corral the palomino snorted. Dropping to his haunches so as to make himself less of a target Coulter drew his gun from its holster. The shuffling was repeated, low but definite. There was no mistaking it, and he thought he knew what it was. It was the almost imperceptible fall of a foot in the dust of the yard and it was coming from round the corner of the building. Flattening himself against the wall, Coulter edged towards the angle of the building. The sound came once more and this time he thought he heard the slight susurration of drawn breath. Being careful not to make a sound himself, Coulter waited till he felt that whoever was there must be almost to the corner of the building and then he quickly stepped forward in order to have the drop on the intruder. For a moment the two men stared at each other and then the man spoke.

'Don't shoot! As you can see, I'm not holding a gun.'

Coulter's finger was already squeezing the trigger when he pulled it back with a gasp.

'Sparrow,' he gasped. 'What in tarnation are you doin' here?'

It was Henry P. Sparrow, the oldster he had met on the stagecoach. Sparrow looked bemused. He stared hard at Coulter before finally seeming to recognize him.

'Coulter!' he murmured.

He had put his hands up in the air and continued to hold them in that position till it suddenly struck

Coulter what a ridiculous situation they found themselves in. Slipping his Colt back into its holster, he told Sparrow to put his arms down.

'I don't know what this is all about,' he said, 'but I guess you could do with a cup of coffee.'

They made their way inside where Coulter poured a fresh mug of coffee and offered it to Sparrow.

'I guess you'd better explain what you're doin' here,' he said when the oldster had drunk it.

'Reckon I could ask you the same question.' Sparrow looked confused but there was no trace of fear about him. He seemed to be quite at ease with regard to the situation he found himself in.

'You go first,' Coulter said.

The oldster took up the cup and finished it off. Then he sat back in the wooden chair, spreading his fingers against its arm.

'OK,' he said. 'I trust you, Coulter. You put up a good show on that stagecoach. Fact of the matter is I'm a Pinkerton agent. I wasn't on the stage for nothin'. In fact, I was on it for the same reason I'm here right now.' He sat up again.

'Tell me, Coulter, what do you know about a man called Reber?'

'I've heard the name mentioned. Other than that, nothin' at all.'

'Without going into a lot of detail, you might say I've been on the track of Reber for quite some time. He was involved in a lot of shady business back in St.

Louis and Chicago, but it was mainly small-time stuff. It was when there got to be a number of stage and railroad hold-ups that I became involved. Certain people lost a lot of money. They approached the agency. Reber dropped out of things for a time and it was only recently that I picked up his trail again. Seems like he got involved with some fancy *hombre* by the name of Roberts and decided to try and make things look a little more legitimate.'

'By way of the Green Gulch and Western Stagecoach Company,' Coulter cut in.

Sparrow looked at him closely. 'You got the picture,' he said. 'Reckon you know more about this than you've been lettin' on.'

Coulter relaxed. There was something about the little man which rang true. In as few words as possible he outlined his involvement in things.

'So neither of us was on that stage by chance,' Sparrow commented when Coulter had finished.

'So what brings you here now?' Coulter said.

'You're right about the loot. I figured it out too and I came to the conclusion that if Roberts was lookin' for a place to hide the money, this might be as good a choice as any.'

'You mean right here on the waystation?'

'Why not? It's a ready-made location and it would be unlikely anyone would think to look here.'

Coulter thought for a moment. 'Guess you're right,' he said. 'I never thought about it for one.'

'However,' Sparrow continued, 'I now have my doubts. Especially if Roberts suggested you make use of the place. Before you arrived I had an opportunity to look around. So far as I can tell there are no traces of a sizeable group of riders having been here recently. I think you'd agree they'd have left sufficient indications if they had been.'

'Yeah. And there are no traces of anyone having been inside either.'

There was silence for a moment.

'How did you get here?' Coulter said. 'I never saw no sign of you either.'

'My horse is tethered some distance away. Now that you mention it I'd better move him round to the corral.' He got to his feet but hesitated before he reached the door.

'What is it?' Coulter asked.

'Well, I'm still a bit puzzled as to why Roberts gave you the use of this place. Could be he's on to you and it's a trap.'

Coulter shrugged. 'The thought had crossed my mind.'

'We need to be careful,' Sparrow said.

While he was gone Coulter was thinking things over in his mind. A sudden doubt had struck him. What if Sparrow was right but Sparrow himself was the danger? The more he thought about it, however, the less likely it seemed. If Sparrow had wanted to kill him he could have done so with ease when he first arrived at the waystation. The manner in which he had appeared gave every indication that he had just arrived on the scene, had observed Coulter's horse and decided to reconnoitre. Getting to his feet, Coulter wandered outside. Night had fallen and the first stars were appearing in the dark blue vault of the heavens. He heard the chink of a horse's harness and then a whinny and the voice of a man whispering low. Shortly afterwards Sparrow appeared carrying his saddle.

'Sure is a fine night,' he commented.

Coulter nodded his agreement. For a moment they stood together looking out on the darkening prairie before going back indoors and shutting the door behind them.

CHAPTER FOUR

Coulter was dreaming a peaceful dream of night-time on the range with a herd of longhorns sleeping in the grass when he suddenly sat up with a start. His reactions were ahead of him and it took him a moment or two to realize where he was – lying on the floor of the waystation with Sparrow in the bunk of the room next door. Although he could detect nothing untoward he reached for his six-guns lying nearby and then listened intently. All he could hear was the blowing of the wind, till there came a sound from the adjoining room and then the voice of Sparrow called.

'Are you awake, Coulter?'

'Yeah, I'm awake.'

The shadowy figure of Sparrow appeared in the doorway.

'I heard horses,' he said. 'Quite a long way off but I heard them.'

Coulter was still listening closely but could detect nothing.

'There!' said Sparrow, raising a finger.

He went over to the door and, opening it a fraction, peered out into the night.

'Wait a moment,' he said.

Coulter was on his feet. From the doorway he watched as Sparrow lay down in the yard and put his ear to the ground.

'No doubt about it,' he said, rising to his knees. 'Riders, maybe half a dozen of them, and they're comin' this way.'

Coulter was dumbfounded. Listen as closely as he might he still could not detect anything. Yet he had woken from his sleep.

'You must have good senses,' he remarked.

'Been around a long time,' Sparrow replied. 'I guess that's why.'

Quickly they made their way back inside.

'There's only one reason a bunch of riders would be out at this time of night,' Sparrow said. 'Looks like we were right to suspect Roberts's motives.'

'We got two choices,' Coulter said, assuming control of the situation. 'Either we stick around and fight, or we clear out and leave them to it.'

'I never backed down from a fight when it was necessary,' Sparrow remarked, 'but one thing the war taught me was the value of a strategic retreat. There's nothin' to be gained by sluggin' it out at this stage.'

Coulter made a mental note of 'at this stage'. There was a lot more to the old-timer than met the eye.

'OK,' he said. 'Let's do that. But I aim to be back tomorrow when that stage arrives.'

'How do you know it will? Maybe that was all part of the set-up.'

'If we can keep out of sight, we might be able to trail this mob back to wherever they're comin' from.'

'That makes sense,' Sparrow responded. 'Now let's get movin'.'

Swiftly they gathered their things and made for the corral. By the time they had saddled up the horses and stepped into leather Coulter could plainly hear the sound of galloping hoofs. Riding out of the corral, they turned in the opposite direction and rode off into the night, travelling in silence apart from the muffled drum of their horses' hoofs and the occasional creak of harness. The sweep of the Milky Way stretched in a line above them and there was a curious luminosity about the night which allowed them to see for a considerable distance. Coulter's only aim was to keep out of sight and hearing of the riders but Sparrow seemed to know the country and to have a better idea about where they were heading. After a time Coulter could discern a line of cottonwoods looking strangely distorted and nearer than they in fact were. Sparrow veered off in their direction and presently they came to the banks of a wide stream. Sparrow rode straight down into the water and Coulter followed. The depth of the stream was deceptive. Glinting in the starlight, it looked like it might be deep but it was only a matter of some eight inches and barely reached their horses' hocks. Slowing to a walk, they moved down the stream for a little way before Sparrow rode out again and drew his horse to a halt in the shadow of some trees. Looking out from the shelter they had a good view of the plain leading back to the waystation.

'We'll lose them,' Coulter said. 'OK, we might be out of sight, but so are they.'

Sparrow looked across at him. 'I got a hunch they'll be passin' this way,' he said. 'Once they've had a chance to look around the waystation and find that it's deserted.'

Coulter didn't ask him why he thought that way. After the incident on the stagecoach and the way he had heard those riders, he was beginning to have a healthy respect for the oldster.

For what seemed a long time they continued to wait there in the shadow of the trees. Neither of them spoke. They were both looking and listening for the night-riders. When Coulter had just about given up, Sparrow held up his hand.

'I thought so,' he said. 'They're comin' this way. Get ready to ride.'

Again Coulter could hear nothing but Sparrow

seemed to have an uncannily clear idea of which way the riders were headed. Coulter was expecting to wait till they appeared but the oldster had other ideas.

'Keep close to me,' he said, 'but don't say anything. Sound carries. They might even pick up the sound of our horses.'

Emerging from the shelter of the trees, Sparrow swung his horse's head round and for a time they moved back the way they had come, parallel to the cottonwoods. Then Sparrow changed direction and they swung out on the open prairie, following a line which took them at an angle across their former path. All the while Coulter strained his ears to catch any sounds from the group who had been pursuing them. Once or twice he thought he heard something but it was hard to be sure that it wasn't just the sound of their own hoofbeats he was picking up on. The night continued to be suffused by a silvery glow which seemed to fall from the skies, and landmarks such as trees and rocks were eerily distinct. They continued riding for some time till Coulter could see a distant line of hills etched sharply against the skyline. He wasn't sure whether they were the hills he had been prospecting with Bragg. He guessed they were a continuation of the same range. The country was becoming much more broken and presently Coulter did hear something, but it wasn't the sound of horses. It was the faint lowing of a cow. At the same moment Sparrow held up his hand and they drew to a halt.

'Wait!' he said.

They sat in silence until Coulter's ears at last registered the sound of galloping hoofs and presently, off to his left, he saw the dim shadowy forms of horsemen.

'We've been followin' a parallel trail,' Sparrow said. 'Seems like there's cattle up ahead.'

'Yeah,' Coulter replied. 'And I think I know whose cows they are.'

He had referred briefly to Harrison in his discussion with the Pinkerton man.

'They ran off a herd when they attacked the Block H. Harrison was gettin' them ready for a drive.'

'Is that so? Then I would guess he would be aimin' for Penitence. It's on the way to becoming a big cowtown.'

'Let's just get up a bit closer. See what else we can find out.'

Coulter was feeling a little disappointed that their pursuit of the riders had not led to discovering their base of operations but this was something. They moved forward again and as the wind changed direction, they picked up the unmistakable smell of the sleeping herd. The riders had disappeared. They must have ridden back into camp.

'Best not go any further,' Sparrow said, 'at least not on horseback. If the owlhoots don't detect us likely the cattle will.'

They dismounted and tethered their horses to some bushes. Coulter was just about to draw his rifle from its scabbard when something made him look quickly round at Sparrow. The oldster's hand was already on the handle of his gun, but he was too late to do anything as a voice behind them in the darkness snapped, 'Don't try anythin'. We got you covered.'

Both of them stood immobile.

'Just take it easy. Move away from the horses and drop your guns.'

Coulter stepped back slowly and, unfastening his gunbelt, threw it to one side. Sparrow did the same.

'Now turn round. Real slow. My friend has an itchy trigger finger.'

They did as the voice directed. Standing in the shadow of some bushes behind them were three men. Coulter's eyes peered through the darkness to catch a clearer sight of them. Suddenly his features relaxed.

'Harrison!' he exclaimed. 'It's me, Coulter.'

He glanced at the other two. One he didn't recognize but the other he did. It was Logan, the foreman of the Block H. He guessed the other was one of the ranch-hands.

'Coulter?' Harrison said in a wondering tone. He took a step closer. 'By Jiminy, it is you.'

Placing his gun back in its holster, he stepped forward, proffering his hand. Coulter took it in his own and the two of them embraced.

'Hell, you never know what you're goin' to find wanderin' loose on the range,' Harrison quipped.

Logan and the other man sheathed their weapons and Coulter introduced the bemused Sparrow. When the first shock of surprise had worn off Coulter looked Harrison squarely in the eye.

'I guess you don't know what happened at the ranch?' he said.

Quickly he told Harrison about the burning of the Block H. Harrison looked grim but seemed to take it well.

'I ain't surprised,' he said. 'When I realized the cattle had been taken I more or less guessed there would be a lot more to it. Just so long as June and Bragg are OK. Are you sure Bragg will pull through?'

'He's as tough as they come,' Coulter said. 'He'll pull through.'

When the explanations had been made, they sat together to decide what they should do next. Harrison and Logan were all for riding down and running off the herd and Coulter was tempted by the proposition. It was the oldster who pointed out another tack.

'What's to be gained?' he questioned. 'We don't know how many of 'em there are. Somebody will probably get hurt. The cows will be scattered all over the range.'

'What are you suggestin'?'

'Think about it. Seems to me it would make a lot more sense to let them drift the herd clear to Penitence. That way they do our job for us and we step in at the end.'

Coulter let out a low laugh. 'Good thinkin',' he said. 'I don't know about the rest of you, but it seems like a good idea to me.'

The others thought it over. Harrison was still for attacking the owlhoots and driving off the cattle. He was angered by the news of what had happened at the Block H but eventually even he began to see the wisdom of the old man's suggestion.

'OK,' he said. 'But it might be an idea for a couple of us to trail them. After all, we're only guessin' they're headed for Penitence, although it's where I aimed to drive the herd.'

Sparrow nodded. 'Can't see any objection to that,' he said.

Coulter turned to Harrison. 'You've got the biggest stake in this,' he said. 'Why don't you and Logan follow the herd? But remember to keep out of sight.'

'What about the rest of you?'

'I got an appointment at the waystation,' Coulter replied.

'That stage ain't likely to turn up,' Sparrow commented.

'Maybe not. But if it does I'll be bound all the way to Penitence too. Assumin' everything goes to plan, I could meet with you boys there.'

It seemed as good an arrangement as any. There were lots of loose ends but they would have to play it by ear. Coulter got his feet.

'I'd better get movin',' he said. 'See you in Penitence.'

Dawn had broken when Coulter arrived back at the waystation. Sparrow had ridden off in the direction of Green Gulch to see what he could find out there and the cowboy, whose name was Hutton, had gone back to Lodesville with a message for June and Bragg. Coulter wasn't sure what to expect. He was coming round to Sparrow's way of thinking and it now seemed unlikely to him that the stage would put in at the waystation rather than carrying on to Green Gulch, but in this he was wrong. Towards noon he saw a cloud of dust and shortly after the stage came rolling into the yard. The driver looked down at Coulter. He seemed peeved about something.

'You the one volunteered to ride shotgun?' he asked.

'Sure am. Name's Coulter.'

The driver didn't reply. Coulter climbed to the seat beside him. The driver gave him one final look, turned his head and spat into the dust and then cracked his whip. The coach lurched out on to the trail and soon picked up speed. Coulter had noticed that there were only two passengers who both looked like drummers. He guessed they would be picking up more people at Green Gulch. The horses strained at their leads and the coach rattled on.

'Nice up here,' Coulter remarked.

The wind was blowing and he felt exhilarated. The coach bumped and swayed and it took something of an effort at times to remain upright, but Coulter was enjoying it. He attempted a couple of other remarks but the driver remained taciturn. Coulter looked at him out of the corner of his eye. He looked about forty but there was nothing distinctive about him. Coulter turned his attention back to the scenery. It seemed to him that they had taken a different trail somewhere and were not heading in the direction of Green Gulch. Turning to the driver once more he put this to him.

'Ain't goin' to Green Gulch,' the driver answered after a time.

'I thought that was the next stop.'

'Usually. Not this time.'

The driver cracked his whip. He seemed even more displeased and Coulter guessed it was because he had been instructed to avoid Green Gulch that he was in a bad mood. Maybe he knew somebody there. Maybe he just welcomed a break.

'So where is the next halt?'

'Big Hat.'

'Never heard of it.'

'That's probably because there's nothin' there less'n you count a hut that passes as the next waystation.'

Coulter was about to ask the reason why they were missing Green Gulch but changed his mind. The driver was giving nothing away. He would find out soon enough.

It was late when they arrived at Big Hat, but Coulter was pleasantly surprised. The driver's bad mood had obviously influenced his description of the place. It looked as though it might at one time have served as some kind of trading post and was quite a substantial building. Smoke from the chimney rose into the night air. There were horses in a corral and a generally lived-in look about it. The horses looked pretty wild. They were mustangs and Coulter wondered what they were doing there till he remembered Roberts's comments about having a ready supply of horses. Obviously Roberts had several strings to his bow and dealing in horseflesh was just another of them.

As the coach swung into the yard and drew to a halt, they were greeted by a big man with a beard. As if in accordance with the name of the place, he wore a Big Four hat.

'Any problems?' he called to the driver, as he opened the door for the two passengers to alight.

'Nope. Got me a shotgun messenger to take care of things.'

The man with the beard looked at Coulter. 'Name's Jameson,' he said. 'I run this place. Don't take a lot of doin'.'

Coulter swung down. Jameson led the way into the building. It looked almost cosy with a fire burning in the grate and a table partly spread with food. There was a big pot of stew brewing over the flames.

'Make yourselves at home,' Jameson said. 'Help yourselves to grub. I'll just attend to the horses.'

Coulter looked around for the two drummers but they weren't there. After a time they emerged from a one of the rooms leading out of the main area. Coulter was surprised at their apparent familiarity with the place, but then turned his attention to the stew which the driver was ladling into a bowl. Taking his turn, he filled his own bowl and sat at the table to eat. The two passengers had taken up chairs near to the fire. Nobody spoke. Presently Jameson reappeared.

'That's the way,' he said. 'It ain't much but I knew you were comin'.'

When they had eaten the two drummers got up and went back into the room they had seemingly acquired for the night. Coulter moved to the veranda and sat down on a seat. He pulled out his pack of Bull Durham and built himself a smoke. After a time he was joined by Jameson who accepted his offer of tobacco. The driver seemed to have retired for the night.

'This your first time ridin' shotgun?' Jameson remarked.

'More or less,' Coulter said.

'Should be a clear run between here and Penitence. But you can never tell. It's a new route. I only took over here myself less than a week ago. Reckon it could be a short appointment.'

'How's that?'

'All depends on whether the line proves successful. Guess the operator's takin' a big risk.'

When he had finished his cigarette Jameson got to his feet.

'Guess I'll be turnin' in,' he said.

After he had gone Coulter continued to sit on the veranda. It was a peaceful evening. He should have been tired after the exertions of the previous night but he felt oddly restless. After a time he stood up and made his way to the corral at the back of the building where the mustangs were gathered, their shapes shadowy against the backdrop of night. Some of them stirred uneasily and one of them approached him, tossing its head and snorting.

'Everything all right with you, old fella?' Coulter said.

His voice sounded strangely loud in the silent landscape. Suddenly he felt uneasy. Behind the corral stood a little grove of trees. He strained his eyes to search its dark and silent depths, but there was nothing he could discern. He began to move round the corral, drawing his gun as he did so. He still could not see or hear anything untoward, and he was beginning to think it was only his nerves. Maybe the activities of the previous night were beginning to catch up with him after all. Maybe it was just his voice breaking the quiet. There was nothing to cause concern. The others were sleeping in the waystation. But he failed to convince himself. A man out here learned to trust his instincts, and his instincts were telling him to be careful.

He had circled the corral and was about to cross the short space of open ground between himself and the trees when he was stopped in his tracks by the crack of a rifle shot. Immediately he hit the ground, rolling over to a position where he could loose a round himself in the direction from which he had seen the stab of flame. Another shot rang out and a bullet thudded into a corral fence post inches above his head. The shot came from a different place among the trees so there must be at least two of them. At the sound of the explosions the horses in the corral took fright and one of them came charging towards him, crashing through a section of the fence. Coulter, realizing he was in a bad position, took his chance and as the horse came by, rose to his feet, grabbed it by the head and managed to swing himself aboard. He was riding bare-back as further shots whistled about him. The charging horse screamed in pain as a bullet scorched across its flanks, but it was clear now of the immediate danger area and Coulter clung on until he was able to slow it down and slide from its back.

He now had the edge. The men were concealed, but they had lost the element of surprise. As far as he was concerned, they had lost their opportunity. He supposed it was just the darkness of the night that had saved him. Who were they? Where had they come from? The waystation was isolated and a long way from anywhere in particular. He began to make his way back to the cabin, aiming to approach the bushwhackers from the side. When he got to the corner of the building he halted and carefully poked his head out so he could see the trees, but there was no indication that anybody was concealed there. He got down on his stomach and inched forward, thinking to crawl the few yards to the shelter of the trees. He had barely started when, turning his head to the right, he could see two figures standing near the corral. He could hardly believe how stupid his attackers were behaving. They must have assumed he had ridden away on the bolting horse. The light was bad and they were standing some distance apart. He might have fired from where he lay, but instead he leaped to his feet, calling out as he did so. Instantly they both turned, but could not immediately locate him. Coulter squeezed the trigger of his Colt Army revolver and saw the nearer figure crumple and fall. The other one fired and lead splattered into the wood of the cabin over Coulter's shoulder. Pivoting, Coulter fired again but missed. The other man began running towards him, firing as he did so. Coulter triggered again and the man fell forwards, impelled by his own momentum before crashing to the earth almost at Coulter's feet.

For a long moment Coulter stood while silence descended, almost as deafening as the noise of firing had been. Then he knelt down and turned the man over. It was one of the men who had been on the stagecoach and who he had thought might be drummers. He had been shot in the head. Coulter stood up and walked slowly over to where the other man lay in the dirt of the corral, blood pouring from his mouth and from a wound in the chest. He was still alive, but as Coulter tried to staunch the bleeding his eyes glazed and he was gone. Coulter recognized him as the other of the two passengers. There was nothing further to be done. Coulter got to his feet and began walking back towards the cabin. As he did so the door burst open and Jameson came running towards him with a gun in his hand closely followed by the stage driver. Seeing Coulter and not realizing who it was in the darkness, he raised his gun.

'Put it down!' Coulter snapped.

For a moment the driver hesitated and then lowered his arm. At the same moment there was a stab of flame from behind him and a bullet went whistling over Coulter's head. Coulter squeezed the trigger of his revolver but the hammer fell on an empty chamber. Without thinking he hurled the weapon in the direction of the driver and dropped to one knee. Jameson, aware for the first time that the driver was behind him but not knowing who he was shooting at, fired again and the driver doubled over before falling first to his knees and then full-length to the floor. Jamming shells into his gun, Coulter rushed forward past Jameson to where the driver lay. Jameson's bullet had caught him square in the chest and he was dead.

'Wait here!' Coulter snapped.

Quickly he ran back to where he had left the bodies in the corral, checking once more that they were dead. He moved to the back of the corral and looked into the bushes but he knew already there was nobody else involved. Returning to where Jameson was standing in the same position he had left him, he briefly explained what had occurred. When he had finished they made their way back to the cabin.

'It must have been a set-up,' Coulter said. 'Those two *hombres* were paid to kill me. Maybe the driver was in on it; I don't know.' For a few moments the thought had occurred to Coulter that Jameson might be in on it too but he quickly put the thought from his mind.

'I still don't get it,' Jameson said.

'I'm not sure I do myself,' Coulter replied, 'but this isn't the first time. The thing that gets me is why they didn't just kill me on the stagecoach?'

'You had the shotgun,' Jameson commented.

'OK, but then why not kill me as I slept.'

'That might have been chancy too. Seems to me you'd be a hard man to creep up on. Maybe you just caught them by surprise. You say you thought you heard somebody down by the corral.'

Coulter looked closely at Jameson. 'I haven't thanked you yet,' he said. 'You probably saved my life out there.'

'Guess it was instinct. To be honest, I thought he was shootin' at me.'

'Well, there's not much to be done till the morning. I don't know about you, but despite what you just said I could sure use some sleep.'

'What you gonna do?'

'I could ask you the same question. Do you plan stayin' on here?'

Jameson was confused. Things had turned out a lot different from what he had expected when he took on the job. Maybe his own skin would be on the line.

'Tell you what,' Coulter said, 'there's still a stagecoach to be got through. When we've buried those varmints why don't we carry on to Penitence?'

'What? Me drivin' and you ridin' shotgun?'

Coulter shrugged. 'Seems a sensible arrangement.' He started for the door and then stopped. 'Hell,' he said. 'I forgot about those mustangs.'

Jameson grunted. 'No need to worry about them. Somebody'll be by to drive them over to Roberts's place tomorrow.'

'What place is that?' Coulter said.

'I don't ask questions,' Jameson answered. 'Seems like he's got some sort of place between here and Green Gulch.'

Coulter stood for a moment turning over what Jameson had been telling him. Then he jerked to attention again.

'Hell, I nearly forgot. There's still a horse loose out there. Better round him up. Who knows, he might even be needed for the six-in-hand.'

Jameson looked perplexed.

'Took a little night ride,' Coulter said. 'Just before you appeared.'

Jameson's look of perplexity changed into a broad smirk.

'Those mustangs is pretty wild,' he said.

'Yeah,' Coulter replied. 'Next time I'll maybe use a saddle.'

Even though he was lying in a comfortable bunk that night, sleep did not come easily to Coulter. His brain was in a whirl trying to puzzle out just exactly what he knew, what was surmise, and above all what to do about the situation. A few things seemed relatively clear. Reber, whoever he was, had been working in cahoots with Roberts. Roberts had double-crossed Reber by organizing the attack on the stagecoach and making off with the money. Some other gunmen, the ones who had shot his dog, were looking for Reber. Maybe they knew about Roberts. Bragg had recognized one of the riders when he had the shootout in the saloon. The marshal had arrested Bragg and he was in Reber's pay. Had the attack on the Block H been carried out by Reber or the gun-slicks who were looking for him? Whoever it was had obviously been looking for Coulter and Bragg. The link had to be Roberts. It must be Roberts who was responsible both for the attack on the stage and the attack on the ranch. Coulter knew the reason for the stagecoach affair, but why the ranch? Because Roberts wanted revenge? Yes, but there was more to it than that. Roberts had seen another opportunity to extend his influence by taking the ranch and the herd. Maybe the outlaws had gone too far in almost destroying the Block H. Maybe that had not been on Roberts's agenda. But he had certainly rumbled Coulter. Perhaps his suspicions had been aroused when Coulter slipped away after the stage incident, or someone had recognized him from the jailbreak. He might not have been too clever in approaching Roberts in the saloon. Whatever it was, that was why he had been targeted. Now Roberts could afford to let Reber fester away in Lodesville, and he could take over the Lodesville end of things in his own time. And then a new thought struck Coulter. Things could get really interesting if Reber were to find out that Roberts had double-crossed him. What would Reber do about it? Whatever the outcome, however, one thing was for sure: Bayard was his. Exhausted with the thoughts buzzing through his head, Coulter fell asleep at last.

CHAPTER FIVE

It was late in the morning when Coulter and Jameson rattled out of the waystation yard in the stagecoach. Nobody had turned up about the mustangs, but Jameson was confident they would. Besides, it was not his problem now. Whether or not it was a scheduled trip, they were resolved to simply push on as quickly as they could, avoiding any of the potential pick-up stops on the way. Too bad if any passengers were waiting. Jameson had been for simply riding to Penitence and leaving the stagecoach out of it, but something at the back of Coulter's mind persuaded him that the stage might still have a role to play. He couldn't say what it was. The whole episode seemed to have been designed to trap him, but it seemed too elaborate. Roberts could have had him removed in some simpler way. He had a feeling there was something else involved, something he was missing. As it was there was a strange feeling of unreality about the ride, as if he and Jameson were mere shades riding a ghost line. There were no passengers, no schedule, no stops. He was riding with a total stranger. What did he know about Jameson? What was he doing at the relay station? Coulter's brain was already tired and overworked with all the thinking he had done the previous night. He resolved to stop trying to explain it and let things work themselves out in their own time, but no sooner had he directed his attention to the country they were passing through than he began to think about June. She was quite a woman. Had she been truly honest with him about her relationship with Rance Germain? Was she over it? He was surprised to find that it worried him. What was she to him after all? He thought about Bragg. Hopefully the big man was well on the road to recovery by now. It would have been good to have him along.

Sitting on his horse screened by a clump of bushes, Vernon Reber with a bunch of his men awaited the stagecoach as it rumbled towards the sluggish, shallow stream which was a branch of the Owl Creek. He had chosen the spot well. From where he was concealed he would have a clear view of the stagecoach and as it emerged from the water, it would be at its most vulnerable.

'How long, boss?' a thin, sallow-faced man next to

him remarked.

'Should be here pretty soon. Just relax, Bayard. After all, I got my information on good authority. This is goin' to be the easiest pickin's we've had in a long whiles.'

He stopped and looked closely at Bayard. 'Less'n you been lyin' to me.'

Bayard flinched and a nerve began to twitch at the corner of his eye.

'Of course I ain't lyin'. Look what happened to the money. Just like I said. Roberts was double-dealin' all the time.'

'You'd better be right. Your story seems to fit. So far that is.'

Reber turned to another rider who was wearing a marshal's badge. 'Better take it off for now, Stringer. Wouldn't want to take the chance of the good citizens of Lodesville findin' out their marshal wasn't all he should be.'

'Ain't no chance of that.'

Reber turned to him with an angry expression on his face. 'Just do as I say,' he snarled.

The man didn't say anything this time but quickly carried out Reber's order. Reber seemed to relent.

'We got us a good setup. I don't want nothin' to get in the way.' He paused and then with an ugly laugh spat into the dust. 'And that goes especially for Norman Roberts,' he added.

The men were silent. The only sounds were the

sighing of the wind and the gentle lap of the water. After a time Reber spat again and as if the mention of Roberts' name had set up an ugly train of thought he suddenly hissed, 'Low-down double-crossin' son of a skunk.'

'I tell you, I'm not lyin',' Bayard began, but Reber quickly silenced him.

'I ain't talkin' about you,' he said, 'I'm talkin' about Roberts. But you'd better not be stringin' me along.'

Again there was quiet. Bayard licked his lips. A line of sweat had gathered on his brow. He had no reason to doubt that he was right about Roberts, but what reason did Reber have for believing the money would be on this stage? If Reber was wrong about this then it wouldn't be himself he would blame.

Any further meditations were stopped by the faint rumbling of wheels. Immediately the attention of everyone was focused on the trail leading down to the stream. A cloud of dust indicated the approach of a vehicle and then the stagecoach came into view.

'OK boys,' Reber hissed. 'This is it.'

He reached for his neckerchief and pulled it up to just below his eyes. The others followed his example. Bayard felt a surge of relief. At least the stage had showed up as predicted: he hadn't been wrong. He drew his rifle from its scabbard as the stagecoach drew nearer. They were all straining their eyes to see who was on it. They could see the driver and the shotgun guard but there didn't seem to be anyone else. On it came at a quick pace, the six horses straining, their hoofs pounding on the dirt track. As the stage neared the approach to the water it slowed slightly but still came down the long slope at a good pace. A few more yards and the lead horses were in the water. The coach rocked slightly as the other horses followed and then the coach was in the stream, a low wave curling up as water slapped halfway up the wheels. The driver cracked his whip as the man riding shotgun fingered his weapon and let his eyes sweep the river-bank. Reber held up his arm and then let it drop. It was the signal to commence firing and, as the stage emerged from the water and began to climb the incline of the near shore, it was met by a hail of gunfire. The lead horses reared and the driver spun round with his hand in the air. The guard opened fire and buckshot ripped into the bushes. Two of the outlaws fell from their horses and another couple had their mounts shot from under them. It was a deadly accurate hail and it took them by surprise. Some of the horses began to rear and caused pandemonium to spread among the others. Calling to his men to follow him, Reber spurred his mount and he rode into the open, firing as he went. As he did so, the team of horses pulling the stagecoach veered away and the coach swayed before toppling over on its side.

Coulter had not been taken unawares and his reactions were instantaneous as he squeezed the trigger of his shotgun almost at the same moment as the bullets from the direction of the trees came slamming into the woodwork of the coach. He saw Jameson spin round and then the next thing he was thrown headlong into the water as the coach crashed. The shock of the impact knocked the shotgun from his hands, but he was unhurt and, as he sought shelter behind the overturned wagon, he drew his Colts and began to fire at the group of horsemen who had emerged from the screening trees. Even as he did so he was struck by the ridiculous thought that he seemed to have no luck as far as stagecoach rides were concerned; he had an inappropriate feeling of *déjà vu* before his mind cleared of everything except fighting for his life. Bullets were thudding into the wood of the stagecoach, sending sharp splinters flying into the air. The lead horseman had turned along the riverbank, thinking to get in the rear of Coulter, but that was his mistake. Taking a careful bead on him, Coulter gently squeezed the trigger of his Colt. For a moment time seemed frozen and then the man threw up his arms and toppled backwards as the horse plunged on. After what seemed a considerable time but in fact was no more than a few seconds, the man got to his feet and began to stagger back towards the trees. As he ran he shouted something to someone coming behind him and the words hung on the air:

'Bayard, over here!'

Coulter's ears caught the words and he instantly sought out the man to whom they were directed. He was riding towards the first man and, as he reached him, he held out an arm and swung the man up behind him. Coulter's attention had been riveted by what was happening. Now he clicked into action, taking aim and firing at the horse. At first nothing happened and Coulter assumed he had missed and then, after plunging a little further along the river-bank, the horse's legs suddenly splayed out from underneath and he want down on his belly. The man who was riding passenger was flung to one side where he lay motionless. The other one, Bayard, staggered to his feet and began to run away from the river towards the safety of the vegetation beyond. Coulter had been so rapt in this cameo of action that he was surprised to hear firing directed at the outlaws coming from both sides of the river. Craning forward, he could see the driver further downstream lying behind a log and shooting towards the trees. On the other side of the stream further firing was taking place and panic was beginning to spread among the gunhawks. Coulter resumed shooting as the return fire started to dwindle. Coulter guessed that the outlaws had been thrown into disarray by the amount of resistance they were meeting and that they had no idea how many people they were up against. Coulter looked back over his shoulder but he could not see who the gunman was on the other side of the stream. A bullet smashed into the stagecoach close to his face and he ducked down. When he looked up again it was to see the remaining outlaws heading back towards the trees. It seemed they had had enough. Coulter didn't need any further encouragement. Getting to his feet and ignoring the odd bullet which still slapped into the water nearby, he splashed his way out of the stream and up the river-bank, looking for Bayard. It was Bayard who had shot his dog and now that fortune seemed to have delivered Bayard into his hands, he didn't intend to let the opportunity slip.

Pausing for breath he glanced up and down the river. He could see the body of the first outlaw lying beside the dead horse, but there was no sign of Bayard. He had been heading for the trees and without further consideration, Coulter plunged in after him. Which way should he go? Straight ahead for the moment. He ran on, his eyes searching for any sight of Bayard among the vegetation. A root caught at his heel and he tripped over but was instantly back on his feet again. Behind him there were sporadic sounds of gunfire, but then they ceased and there was only the quiet rustling of the leaves. He continued running till the woods began to thin. They didn't extend very far back and soon he had emerged into more open country with stands of timber. His eyes searched the landscape. Which way should he go? There was still no sign of Bayard. He swore with frustration but the man couldn't be far. The next moment he was made aware of this as the report of a rifle rang out close at hand and a bullet went singing over his head. Without a thought for his own safety Coulter began to move towards the sound. Another shot blasted and this time he saw the stab of flame coming from some bushes off to his right. Something had taken possession of Coulter and he had only one thought now repeating itself over and over in his brain. Bayard had killed his dog and now he would kill Bayard. A roaring sound seemed to fill his ears and ahead of him the landscape seemed to have narrowed to a point where he knew the gunman was concealed. It was as though he had tunnel vision. Running as hard as he could, he flew over the ground between him and the bushes, oblivious of the bullets that went whistling by him. Something caught at his sleeve but he crashed on.

Suddenly the bushes to his left parted and Bayard emerged running fast, turning to fire as he did so. Coulter fired in return and then squeezed the trigger for a second shot but the hammer fell on an empty chamber. Hurling the gun in the direction of his quarry he charged on. He was gaining ground when Bayard suddenly took a tumble. He was on his feet again in an instant, but not before Coulter had made up the remaining ground and thrown himself headlong at his adversary. He caught him round the legs and as Bayard fell, Coulter reached out his hand to grab his opponent's gun hand. They lay kicking and sprawling in the dirt, each trying to gain control of the weapon. Coulter had the upper hand, however, and as Bayard struggled to raise his gun hand, Coulter smashed it back against the ground and the gun fell loose. Before Coulter could take advantage Bayard had caught him with a knee to the crotch and as a wave of pain engulfed him his hold loosened and Bayard was on his feet, bending down to get the gun. Blindly, Coulter kicked out and caught Bayard in the midriff. As he doubled over Coulter smashed a fist against his chin and Bayard rocked backward. Coulter stepped forward but Bayard side-stepped him and the next instant Coulter saw a flash of light and there was a knife in Bayard's hand.

'I don't know who you are,' Bayard said, 'but I'm sure gonna enjoy carvin' you in pieces.'

He lunged forward, but Coulter stepped deftly to one side. Nevertheless the sharp curved blade sliced through a sleeve of his jacket and he felt a sharp pain in his left arm. Bayard began to circle Coulter, hefting the knife from hand to hand as he did so. Suddenly he ran forward and this time Coulter was too slow. He had expected Bayard to stab at him with his right hand but it was the left that carried the knife and Coulter winced as he felt it slide across his upper leg. Instantly changing his grip, Bayard came at him again. Coulter ducked low and, as Bayard's arm described a circle over his head, he butted him in the stomach. Bayard gasped and staggered backwards. Seizing the initiative, Coulter rushed at him again and this time they both went over together. Bayard was the first to recover and he flung himself on top of Coulter who raised his arm just in time to grasp Bayard's knife hand as it was about to descend. Now Coulter was at a real disadvantage and he needed all his strength to resist Bayard's downward pressure. Bayard sensed victory as slowly but surely the knife came down till the point was almost in Coulter's face. With a last effort born of sheer desperation Coulter found a final reserve of strength and forced Bayard's hand upwards for an inch and then another. Arching his back, Coulter managed to kick out and Bayard rolled to one side. He was up quicker than his opponent and as Coulter struggled to regain his feet he ran at him with the knife raised to strike. Coulter ducked and Bayard went over him. Coulter turned but Bayard was not moving. Coulter was confused and moved forward to kick his opponent in the ribs when he saw a line of blood flowing from beneath Bayard who was lying on his stomach. Pausing for just a moment to make sure he was not bluffing, Coulter kneeled down and turned him over. Bayard's eyes looked up at him with an expression of pain and bewilderment. His lips moved but Coulter couldn't hear what he was saying. He put his head down to catch the man's feeble whisper.

'Who are you?' he breathed.

Coulter didn't know what to reply. Looking down, he saw the knife which was protruding from Bayard's belly. He had landed on it when he fell. Untying his neckerchief, Coulter folded it and held it against the wound, trying to stanch the flow of blood.

'It's no use,' the man groaned.

His eyes clouded over and then his head fell back. Coulter got to his feet. He felt empty and cold. The world which had speeded up while he was chasing the outlaw and seeking revenge began to slow. He became aware of the sun shining low over the tree-tops, of drifting clouds and the fluting of a bird. For a few moments he couldn't think what he was doing there and then the memory of recent events flooded back to his brain and he started forward to find out what had happened to Jameson and the stagecoach. He wasn't sure what to expect but he feared the worst. As he came through the woods he heard someone shouting his name and then he was surprised to see a figure coming towards him. His hand automatically reached for the gun he had thrown aside and then he stopped in his tracks, staring with disbelief. The man coming towards him was Sparrow!

'Coulter!' Sparrow was shouting. 'Are you OK?'

Coulter ran forward. 'I'm all right,' he confirmed. 'But what about Jameson? They shot him but I saw him in the water. He was firing at the outlaws.'

'Jameson took a slight hit but he'll be fine.'

The two of them made their way through the trees till they emerged on the river-bank. The stagecoach was still lying in the water but the horses had been freed. Sitting propped up against a log was Jameson with his arm in a sling.

'Coulter!' he called. 'We thought they'd got you.'

The three of them collapsed on the grass and soon the story of what had happened was told. Jameson had been hit in the shoulder and flung into the water when the stagecoach toppled over, but had got into a position where he could return fire. The situation would have been lost, though, if Sparrow hadn't arrived on the scene and it was apparent why the man had survived as a Pinkerton agent.

'When I left Coulter after we came on the herd,' he said, 'I made my way to Green Gulch. I heard some talk about Roberts. I got to thinkin' about things and it seemed to me Coulter was puttin' his head right back in the noose when he set off for the waystation. I figured the best thing I could do would be to get back there. Of course I found the place deserted but it was easy enough to pick up your trail.'

'You got here in the nick of time,' Jameson commented.

'I figure those varmints were caught by surprise. They probably reckoned there were more than just me. All the same, they didn't seem to put up much of a show.'

'I think you'll find that body lyin' by the horse on the river-bank is Reber,' Coulter said. He had told them about his encounter with Bayard but hadn't gone into any detail. He was beginning to have some mixed feelings about the way events were turning out. He didn't feel the way he thought he would after he had caught up with the man who killed his dog.

'What I can't quite figure,' Sparrow said, 'is why those varmints decided to attack the stage. I was thinkin' it might be part of Roberts's plan to get rid of Coulter, but somehow that don't quite seem to add up.'

'Yeah, I was thinkin' the same,' Coulter said. 'Those two coyotes who crept up on me at the waystation were out to get me. If they'd succeeded there would have been no call for this show.'

'If it wasn't Coulter they was after, what other reason would they have for drygulchin' the stage?' Jameson put in.

'Maybe they thought it was carryin' somethin',' Sparrow suggested.

Coulter had passed round his pouch of Bull Durham. Now they sat beside the wreckage of the stage and enjoyed the satisfying hit of the tobacco.

'I been thinkin',' Coulter said. 'Even before all this happened. Sure, those two varmints at the waystation were out to kill me, but maybe there was more to it than that. They seemed to know their way around the place. What were they doin' out in the bushes that night? They couldn't have known I was goin' to take a walk just then. So maybe they were out for some other reason. Maybe I disturbed them but they thought they'd take their chance anyway and get rid of me.'

Sparrow sat up, suddenly animated. 'I think you could be on to somethin',' he said. 'But what could they have been up to?'

'Roberts keeps those wild horses there in the corral,' Jameson said. 'It was one of my duties to keep an eye on 'em. Could there be a link there somehow?'

'In a way,' Coulter said. 'At the very least it shows that Roberts has been makin' use of the place.'

'Yeah. And Roberts needed somewhere to hide that loot he arranged to be taken from the stage. Somewhere Reber might not know too much about. How about if he had it stacked away somewhere at the waystation?'

'And maybe those two owlhoots who tried to kill you were there to collect it and take it on by stage to

Green Gulch, or wherever else Roberts might have in mind. Like I said, these owlhoots had to have a reason for ambushin' the stage and we've already decided the reason wasn't to kill Coulter.'

They looked at each other with a dawning understanding in their eyes.

'It makes sense,' Sparrow said. 'After all, I thought they might have stashed it away at the other waystation. Leastways, I think we should act on it.'

'You mean get back to Big Hat and start lookin' for the loot?'

Sparrow nodded.

'We'd better get movin' on it quick,' Coulter said. 'Before Roberts gets there. Once the stage doesn't show up where it's meant, he'll soon put two and two together.' He turned to Jameson. 'Can you manage it?' he said.

Jameson laughed. 'Sure. Takes more than this to stop me. It's just a flesh wound. Looks worse than it is.'

Sparrow got up and walked to where his horse was tethered after he had collected it from across the stream.

'Let me take a closer look,' he said. 'I done a bit of doctorin' on the side.'

By the time he had finished Jameson was looking a lot better. Night was falling but they decided to make a move. Coulter and Jameson chose a couple of the stagecoach's team of horses and then, slapping their rumps, sent the others off to find their own way. After replenishing their armaments from what the outlaws left behind, they mounted and started the ride back to the waystation.

It was late as they approached Big Hat and they were surprised to see that there was a light in the window and smoke curling from the chimney.

'What do you make of it?' Sparrow said.

'Whoever it is they don't seem to mind advertising their presence,' Coulter replied.

'It can't be Roberts; even if he realizes by now that the stagecoach isn't comin' he wouldn't have had time to get here yet.'

'Could be one or two of the varmints we just fought off,' Jameson suggested. 'Made their way here.'

'Reber probably didn't even know this place existed,' Coulter said, 'but we'd better take care.'

Leaving their horses tethered to some bushes they moved forward on foot. As they drew near to the building they spread out, Sparrow and Jameson veering to the side while Coulter approached directly. When he was satisfied that the other two were in position, Coulter crept forward so as to peer through the window. Before he had reached his target the door opened and a figure appeared silhouetted against the light. It was dark; there was only one lamp burning within the building and it was hard at first to make out who the figure was.

Coulter, crouching in the shadows below the porch, reached slowly for his gun. As he did so the figure moved and Coulter could see who it was. Before he could do anything a voice called from within the room.

'Everything OK, June?'

She turned back.

'Sure, everything's fine. Thought for a moment I heard somethin' but it was probably just a rat.'

If Coulter had been surprised to see June, he was even more surprised at the sound of the man calling from within. It was the voice of Bragg. His first instinct was to stand up and reveal himself but he didn't want to take June by surprise and alarm her or Bragg into doing something rash. He glanced along the building and could just see Sparrow's face peering out from a corner of the building. It was an awkward situation.

'Come back inside,' Bragg's voice continued.

The woman turned and, with a last glance, re-entered the building. As the door closed behind her Coulter rose to his feet and signalled the others to come to him, trusting that they could make out his gestures in the dark. They were with him in a trice and moving back a little way, he told them who it was within the cabin.

'What in tarnation are they doin' here?' Jameson asked.

'I don't know. More to the point, how do we

announce our presence without spookin' 'em?'

Sparrow grinned. 'The answer's easy,' he said.

His two companions turned to him in the dark.

'That cowboy from the Block H. I can't remember his name but he left for Lodesville after we flushed out those rustlers with the herd.'

'Hutton,' Coulter said. 'That was his name. Of course, I sent a message back with him.'

'And all we have to do right now is just ride in same as anyone would and make ourselves known.'

Returning to their horses, they mounted up and rode to the waystation.

'Ho there!' Sparrow called as they approached the yard.

The door opened and this time it was Bragg who appeared with a rifle in his hands. He looked up at them and was about to say something when he realized one of the riders was Coulter.

'Coulter!' he exclaimed, and turning his head, called to June. In a second she was by his side. Coulter had swung down from the leather and the three of them were holding each other.

'Let me introduce a couple of friends of mine,' Coulter said.

When the introductions were over they all made their way into the waystation and it wasn't long before June had made a pot of coffee and they were sitting and making their explanations. Hutton, the Block H ranch hand, had indeed passed on the message from Coulter and, getting concerned about what might be happening, Bragg and June had decided to leave Lodesville and follow Coulter's tracks.

'But when I left, you weren't in any fit state to be doin' anythin',' Coulter said to Bragg.

Bragg grinned. 'Guess I had a good nurse.'

'He didn't need much nursing,' June interposed quickly. 'He must have the constitution of a buffalo.'

'Anybody been here since you arrived?' Jameson enquired.

'Nope. Was somebody expected?'

'A couple of Roberts's men. About the horses.'

'We fed 'em ourselves. There was some feed in a hut back of the corral. They seemed to be gettin' restless. No wonder.'

Jameson thought about it for a moment or two.

'I guess that means there'll be visitors tomorrow.'

'Especially now that Roberts must realize somethin' has gone wrong with his plans.'

They lapsed into silence. It was getting quite late when Sparrow returned to the subject of the money.

'So you figure Roberts arranged for it to be taken here after the hold-up?' Bragg said.

'It's only a guess, but it makes a lot of sense.'

They all looked at one another.

'What are we waitin' for?' Sparrow said. 'Let's get searchin'. If necessary we can turn this place upside down.'

'Before we go that far,' Coulter said, 'let's just think for a moment. My guess is that those two coyotes who tried to kill me were outside looking for the chest with the loot when I disturbed them. If I'm right, that means it's somewhere outside, somewhere back of the corral. Maybe we should start lookin' there.'

'It's dark,' Jameson said. 'Perhaps we should wait till mornin'.'

It was a sensible suggestion and people were inclined to go along with it till Coulter intervened.

'By this time Roberts will know that somethin's gone wrong. Quite apart from any issues with the mustangs, that means he'll be headed this way at the earliest opportunity and he'll be bringing his gang of gunslicks with him.'

They considered this.

'Coulter's right,' Sparrow said, 'we ain't got much time. And if that's the case, we'd better do somethin' about fortifying this place. Better get ourselves organized for a fight.'

'Maybe it would be best to leave,' Coulter said.

He was thinking of the danger to June, but it was June herself, sensing his concern, who answered him, speaking for the others as she did so.

'You can forget that idea,' she retorted. 'Now we've come this far none of us is thinking about turning back.' She looked to Coulter and Bragg. 'Besides,' she added, 'the only way we can get on the right side of the law ourselves is to deal with Roberts once and for all.'

'Reber was the man responsible for getting the marshal on our backs,' Coulter said, 'but I take your point.'

'You figure the marshal was ridin' with the gunslicks who bushwhacked you?' Bragg said.

'I reckon he probably was.'

He had told Bragg about Reber but had given only the flimsiest account of his showdown with Bayard. Now he felt a certain revulsion at the whole business and he gave voice to something he had been considering.

'Maybe this whole affair can be settled without more bloodshed,' he remarked.

Bragg looked at him with a puzzled expression on his countenance.

'Yeah?' he said. 'How d'you figure that one out?'

'I'm aimin' to ride out and meet Roberts. Perhaps I can persuade him to come to some sort of terms.'

June gave a low gasp and Coulter was surprised by the look almost of anguish on her face.

'No,' she said, 'you can't do that. It would be too dangerous.' She turned to the others for support. 'Tell him,' she said. 'Tell him not to be so foolish.'

They looked a little embarrassed. Sparrow turned to Coulter.

'She's right. A man like Roberts ain't likely to listen to reason. He's already tried to kill you more than once.'

'It's still worth a try,' Coulter said.

'Let me come with you,' Bragg volunteered.

Coulter shook his head. 'Nope,' he said. 'I appreciate your offer, but somethin' like this is best left to one man alone. Don't worry; I can take care of myself.'

Bragg gave him a long look before shrugging his shoulders. The others were silent and seeing that there was not much else she could do to persuade them to her view of the matter, June turned and flounced from the room. There was silence for a few moments till Sparrow spoke up again.

'OK,' he said. 'What about we start lookin' for that loot?'

Following Coulter's suggestion, they made their way outside. The night was clear with a host of stars and a bright moon. The mustangs were restless at their approach so they gave them as wide a berth as they could as they made their way to the trees behind the corral.

'You say it was here that you saw those two varmints?' Jameson said.

'Yeah. You came out of the building and came on the stagecoach driver from that direction,' Coulter recapped.

'We ain't got much chance of finding the chest if it's buried in the woods somewhere,' Jameson replied, 'although I never seen no sign of any diggin' since I been here. We'll need shovels. Maybe there'll be some sign where the ground's been disturbed but we ain't goin' to see much in this light.'

There was no reply from Coulter. He had stopped in his tracks and now he ran his fingers through his hair.

'Hell,' he said, 'we're bein' so stupid. The answer is right in front of us.'

'How do you mean?' Bragg said.

'What was that you said about feedin' the horses?'

Bragg shrugged. 'Just that they seemed unsettled and we fed 'em on some grain we found in a shed back among the trees.' He stopped suddenly and the others looked at Coulter with a light dawning in their eyes.

'The shed!' Bragg exclaimed. 'You figure the loot is stacked away in the shed!'

'Where else?' Coulter said.

Bragg had already started off. The others followed close behind and it was only a matter of a few moments before the shed loomed up out of the gloom. They rushed forward and pulled up outside the door which was hanging open.

'Was it like this when you found it?' Coulter asked Bragg.

'Yes. I never gave it any thought.'

'If Roberts had stored his loot in there, he would surely have locked the door.'

'Remember that Roberts wasn't here in person to supervise. Maybe his gang were just careless. Maybe they didn't even know what was in the box.'

'Let's get inside and stop arguin',' Sparrow said. 'Maybe the bullion's still in there.'

They stepped inside. Jameson had brought a lamp and, as he turned up the wick, it revealed bare walls and a dirt floor upon which stood a number of sacks containing grain. Some of the sacks had been ripped open and grain had spilled out. There was nothing else.

'If there's anythin' hidden in here, it's got to be in the grain sacks,' Coulter said.

'Guess so,' Sparrow replied. He strode over to one of the open sacks and, turning it upside down, poured the rest of its contents on the floor.

'If it's in one of those sacks, you'll feel the weight,' Coulter said.

Sparrow turned to the next sack when suddenly the door slammed. For a moment, taken by surprise, nobody moved and then as one they sprang for the door. Coulter rattled the handle. The door was locked from the outside. They looked at each other in frustration.

'What fools we've been,' Coulter snapped. 'One of us should have kept an eye on that door. Especially when we found it unlocked.'

'Shoulda guessed somethin' was wrong.'

They shoved at the door again but it was no use.

'Let's take another look,' Jameson suggested. 'Maybe there's some other way.'

It didn't take them long to look the place over. They kicked aside the bags of grain but there was nothing underneath, no sign of a trapdoor.

'Hell,' Coulter said. 'Looks like there's nothin' in those sacks either. Looks like someone got here before us. Maybe we even disturbed them when we arrived.' They began to move back towards the door when suddenly from somewhere outside there came a scream.

'June!' Coulter gasped.

Spurred to renewed efforts they began to kick at the door and rush at it using their shoulders as a battering ram. Coulter's ears were tuned for any repetition of the scream, but there was none. Just as they were winding down their attack on the door Coulter held up his hand for quiet.

'Hold it,' he said. 'Thought I heard something.'

They could hear the horses in the corral and then to Coulter's intense joy and relief the voice of June calling his name.

'In here!' he shouted. 'The hut behind the corral.'

Seconds later there was a shuffling of feet outside and as Coulter drew his gun the lock clicked and the door swung open. Standing outside was June and with her were Harrison and Logan. For a few moments both sets of people looked at each other in amazement and then Harrison broke into a laugh which was immediately followed by a hoot from his foreman.

'Well I'll be a goldurned horny toad if we ain't caught us as nice a bunch of galoots as you'll find this side of the Rockies,' he shouted.

The freed inhabitants of the hut looked at one another sheepishly. They were feeling more than a little foolish but then they began to see the humour of the situation and started laughing too.

'What in tarnation are you doin' here?' Coulter said. 'I thought you were supposed to be followin' the herd to Penitence.'

'Herd's safe. Hutton came back with a couple of the boys from the Block H. We figured we had enough to take over from those rustlin' coyotes when most of them rode out anyway. Made it real easy. One of the varmints spilled the beans about this place so here we are. Me and Logan that is.'

They had stepped outside the hut and were gathered near the corral in the moonlight. June was beside Coulter and without thinking he had put his arm around her. Harrison turned to her.

'Sorry to scare you, lady,' he said. 'But we didn't know just what to expect.'

'It's OK,' she said. 'I'm just so relieved it wasn't somebody else.'

'Roberts, you mean?' Jameson said. 'Don't worry; he'll be here by and by.'

It wasn't till they were back in the waystation building that Sparrow raised the matter that was in all their minds.

'Was it you that got to that hut before us?' he said. 'We found the door open.'

Harrison grinned and exchanged glances with Logan.

'Sure was. And if it's the bullion you're worried about, we found it right there in one of those sacks.' He turned to address them all. 'Take a look,' he said.

Pulling aside a tattered cloth from something in the corner of the room he revealed the chest that Coulter had last seen being removed from the stage by Roberts's gang of gunslicks. The chest was open and laid out neatly inside were stacks of bills.

'Dang my hide!' Jameson exclaimed. 'Is that loot for real?'

'It's all there,' Harrison added. 'Leastways I guess it is. Ain't had time to count it all yet.'

'Hell, what does anyone do with a stash like that?' Logan said.

'More to the point, where did it come from?' Bragg remarked.

Sparrow stepped forward. 'You got a point there,' he said. 'I reckon it musta took a lot of hold-ups and robberies to acquire that sort of collateral. I been trackin' that skunk Roberts for a long time but I never figured on anythin' like this. A lot of people are goin' to be thankful to you folks. Reckon you might come in for a reward.'

'The only reward I want is settlin' with Roberts,' Coulter said. 'One way or the other.'

His arm was still around June and for some reason he pulled her closer to him. He felt her respond and fell to reflecting on whether what he had just said was strictly true.

CHAPTER SIX

As dawn lit the sky, Coulter awoke and started to prepare for his mission. Early as it was, June was up before him to prepare breakfast.

'I'm sorry for last night,' she said. 'I was upset. I just don't want anything to happen to you.'

'Try to understand,' he began, touched by her concern, but she shook her head.

'I can't understand,' she replied. 'There's no use in trying to persuade me otherwise.' There were tears in her eyes.

'Please,' she said, 'Don't go.'

For a moment Coulter was almost persuaded and it took all of his resolve to resist her. Finally he shook his head. Before he could say anything further June turned and left the room. Just then Sparrow emerged from one of the back rooms.

'I still think you're making a mistake,' he said.

'You could be right, but I'll take the chance.'

'Be careful,' Sparrow added. 'Don't expect anything from Norman Roberts.'

'You make sure everything's organized here,' Coulter said. 'I'll be back.'

As Coulter and Sparrow walked out the door and stood for a few seconds in the yard, June reappeared. She had made a big effort to keep a grip on herself and not let her feelings show.

'Make sure you do come back,' she said.

Coulter made to move towards her but he felt awkward and couldn't find the words he wanted to say. Instead he only nodded and stepped into leather. Checking his Colts and the shotgun nestling in its scabbard, he rode out of the yard, not looking back but instead tried to concentrate his attention on the task before him.

He didn't expect anything from Roberts either. The man had been pursuing him with a ruthless persistence and he wasn't likely to change now. If anything, he would want Coulter out of the way more than ever. But Coulter still had the feeling that although it was a hopeless quest, he needed to make this last attempt to resolve the matter in a way that might avoid unnecessary bloodshed. He couldn't help his thoughts straying towards June. He had been guilty of putting her in a position of danger, not just now but ever since he had met her. For a moment or two he was lost in a reverie of how it might be if he had someone like June alongside him and he failed to observe until it was almost too late two riders coming out of a stand of pine. Cursing himself for letting his attention waver, Coulter dug in his spurs and began to ride in the opposite direction. The riders might not represent a threat, but then Roberts was out to get him and must have warned his men to be on the lookout for him. The two men started in pursuit, but Coulter had a lead and his mount was a good one. One of the men shouted something but it was lost in the rush of wind as the palomino raced away. Next moment Coulter was left in no doubt as to the men's intentions as a shot rang out, and then another. The distance was too great and he was moving too fast for the shots to present any problem, but Coulter needed to lose his pursuers. He didn't feel inclined to get mixed up in a shootout at this stage. That might come, but all he wanted for the moment was to get to Roberts with as little trouble as possible.

He was still gaining ground from his pursuers and feeling comfortable when suddenly the situation changed. From Coulter's left another couple of riders appeared and then, ahead of him, he could see the dust of a large group of horsemen. He pulled on the reins and veered away from the newcomers, but out of the dust ahead a group of a dozen or more riders began to emerge. They had seen him too and, as the main bunch continued coming towards him, a few others moved to cut off any avenue of escape.

Coulter was beginning to run out of options. There could be no doubt that these were Roberts's bunch of gunslicks heading towards the waystation. Coulter realized that they had him cornered. There was no point in trying to evade them. He was angry with himself for being careless, but then he reflected that he had come out here in the first place to meet Norman Roberts. This wasn't quite what he had in mind, but he would have the opportunity now to speak to Roberts. On the other hand, shots had been fired at him. He had no option. He drew his horse to a halt and taking out his tobacco pouch, commenced to roll a cigarette. The first two riders came up alongside him. They had guns in their hands.

'Get down off your horse and unbuckle your gunbelt!' one of them snapped.

Coulter did as he was ordered. While he was doing this the main group of riders had approached. In the lead was a big burly man wearing a dark suit and a garish waistcoat. It was Norman Roberts riding a tall sorrel and sporting a fancy rimfire saddle.

'Coulter,' he said in his oddly high-pitched voice. 'I'm real pleased to meet you again.'

Coulter remained silent. He drew on his cigarette and blew smoke into the air.

'Drop that quirly and show some respect when you're spoken to,' someone barked.

'It's all right,' Norman Roberts said. 'Let him enjoy his smoke. It'll be his last.'

The others chuckled. Coulter drew on the cigarette once more and then dropped it, crushing it under his boot.

'Don't mean to show no disrespect,' he said. 'Fact is, I was riding out this way in the hope of meeting you.'

'I'd say that was a mite foolish, wouldn't you?' Roberts retorted.

'Maybe so,' Coulter said. 'But I figured it was the least I could do to return your courtesy calls.'

Roberts grinned. 'You've proved somewhat elusive,' he said. 'I should have dealt with you from the start.'

'Let's not beat about the bush,' Coulter replied. 'You know what I'm here for. I know where the loot's been stacked. I know all about you and Reber. I've got enough on you to put you behind bars for a long time.'

'Try telling that to the marshal,' Roberts retorted.

One of the riders coughed. 'Why don't you just let me finish him off now?'

Roberts turned to him. 'Don't worry,' he said. 'We're going to finish him off all right, but I figure just shooting him would be too easy. What do you boys think?'

A burst of laughter broke out.

'What you got in mind?' someone shouted.

'I think we might have ourselves a bit of fun right here and now before we deal with the rest of 'em.

This sure is going to be some sort of day.'

'There's no necessity,' Coulter began, but got no further. At a signal from Roberts a lariat suddenly snaked out and Coulter found himself pinioned.

'All right,' Roberts shouted. 'Make sure he's fastened tight.'

Roberts's words were greeted by further guffaws and whoops from the group. A couple of riders swung down and, despite Coulter's efforts lashed him tight and tied him to the cantle of Roberts's saddle.

'OK, boys!' he shouted. 'Let's take us a ride.'

If he hadn't already realized the futility of ever hoping to reason with Roberts, Coulter realized it now. With a sickening lurch of his stomach, he understood too the gravity of his situation. With a loud shout accompanied by whoops of delight from his bunch of owlhoots, Roberts dug his spurs into his horse's flanks. The rawhide lariat tightened and Coulter was dragged across the ground. The grass was almost up to the sorrel's fetlocks and initially Coulter felt little pain, but as the horse picked up pace he began to bounce and jolt and it soon seemed like every muscle and bone in his body was aching. His shirt was torn open and the grass scorched his arm and shoulder. He tried to raise his head to help prevent injury, but he couldn't do much to stop his skull banging against the ground. Roberts's men were enjoying themselves and Coulter was fearful of being mangled beneath the hoofs of their horses as they rode round and about him, in and out, whooping and shouting all the while. Coulter was bleeding and cut in various places and his body called out in agony. He struggled to remain conscious but blackness was beginning to descend when suddenly the ground ceased to hurtle by beneath him and he came to a jerking halt. Roberts reined in his horse and turned in the saddle.

'Hope you enjoyed the ride!' he shouted.

The blackness began to disperse as Coulter gritted his teeth against the pain.

'This is the end of the trail, Coulter,' Roberts continued. He turned to his men. 'Unfasten him and get him to his feet. I think it's time we put him out of his misery. Mose, get a rope and put it round that there tree.'

'A necktie party!' someone yelled. 'I sure enjoy me a good hangin'.'

Coulter was dragged to his feet. The lariat was unfastened but his hands were tied behind his back. Looking up, he saw that they had arrived in the shadow of a tall oak tree. A number of hands hauled him underneath an overhanging branch and a knot was fastened around his neck.

'Yup, looks like this is finally it,' Roberts quipped. 'Sure has been nice meetin' you.'

'I can promise you won't get away with this,' Coulter spluttered, but he knew his case was hopeless. This was where it ended. Roberts had won.

'Get him up on a horse,' Roberts commanded.

Coulter was seized by the arm and shoulders and his foot placed in a stirrup. He looked up at the sky. It was blue and cloudless. At least he could carry that image with him. He thought of June Campbell. At the same moment he heard a loud crack. It seemed it must be his own battered body, but instantly it was succeeded by other cracks and Coulter became aware that the sounds were outside him. It was rifle fire he could hear. For a moment there was confusion among Roberts's men. Trying desperately to pull himself together and take advantage of the situation, Coulter removed his foot from the stirrup and went slumping to the ground. He looked up to see one of Roberts's gunhawks standing over him with a pistol in his hand. He braced himself for the shot but it didn't come. Instead he saw a look of surprise and pain spread across the gunman's features as he sagged heavily to the grass, a gaping wound pumping blood from his chest.

'Coulter!' a voice called.

It was Bragg and the next moment Bragg himself was beside him, cutting at his bonds with a knife.

'Bragg!' Coulter gasped. 'What's happening?'

'No time to go into all that now,' Bragg said. The rope frayed and split. Coulter began to rub his hands and legs.

'Do you think you can ride?' Bragg asked.

'Sure, just give me a few moments.'

The sounds of battle had ceased and Coulter looked around. Several of Roberts's men lay on the ground, dead or dying. The rest of them had ridden off. Bragg stood beside him and back of him he could now see a group of others, among whom he recognized Sparrow, Harrison, and June.

'How did you manage to get here?' he said.

'Sparrow was never happy about your plan to meet Roberts,' Bragg replied. 'None of us was. Seemed sensible to follow behind. Lucky we got here.'

'And just in the nick of time. They were about to lynch me.'

There was a sudden movement behind Bragg and June rushed forward, throwing herself into Coulter's arms.

'What have they done to you?' she sobbed.

Coulter began to utter his thanks to all of them when suddenly his legs seemed to give way beneath him and he sank to the ground.

'Better get him back to the relay station,' Sparrow said. 'He's about done.'

'Looks like they weren't after just hanging him,' Jameson said, joining the group. He held out the lariat. 'Looks to me like he's been dragged.'

June was sobbing as the others helped lift Coulter into the saddle.

'They won't leave it at this,' Sparrow said. 'They'll be back.'

Forcing himself into awareness, Coulter sat up.

'I reckon we need to get back double quick and prepare ourselves. Roberts will be rounding up the rest of his honchos, and then he'll hit us hard. Better get ready for a showdown.'

Quickly they all remounted and began the ride back to the waystation. Coulter slumped in the saddle and winced at each movement of his horse. He felt faint but knew he must just hold on for a little longer. Fortunately it was not far. As they rode into the yard Logan ran out to meet them.

'Any trouble back here?' Sparrow rapped.

'No, but it sure looks like you been hittin' some.'

'Help me get Coulter down,' June ordered.

Together with Sparrow she helped Coulter out of the saddle and then they supported him through the door and into one of the bedrooms where they lay him down gently on the bed and removed his torn garments. June fetched water and began to clean him up. She sobbed as she saw what Roberts had done to him.

'I just can't bear to think about it,' she said.

'Don't think; I'll survive.'

'Thank God we got there when we did.' She shivered. 'Another few minutes and it might have been too late.'

Harrison appeared in the doorway with a bowl of broth.

'This might help,' he said.

June helped to spoon it down Coulter's throat as Sparrow entered the room.

'How's he doing?' he asked.

Coulter himself answered. 'Just give me a bit of time,' he said. 'I'll be fine.' He lay back.

'I don't know how long we'll have before Roberts and his gunmen get here. Not very long I should think. Let me rest up while you do everything you can to secure the place, but wake me the second there's any sign of them.'

'You're not in a condition to do anything,' June said.

'I will be,' Coulter retorted. 'Just wake me when the time comes.' He managed a wry smile. 'After all this you don't think I'd miss out on the final show, do you?'

June leaned across and kissed him and then, drawing the curtains, left the room with the others. For a few moments Coulter lay in the darkened room feeling the pain of his injuries, then lapsed into a deep sleep. When he came round June was beside him.

'How long have I been out?' he asked.

'A couple of hours, maybe more.'

'Any sign of Roberts?'

She shook her head. 'I guess he had to round up some more of his men, but it can't be long now till he gets here.'

He struggled to sit up. His head swam and he had

a thumping headache. June tried to dissuade him.

'I'm OK,' he said. 'Just give me a minute or two.'

He sat on the edge of the bed and then hauled himself to his feet. He was a little groggy but the feeling passed. He felt stiff and sore all over. There was a knock on the door.

'How are you?' Sparrow said.

Coulter repeated what he had just told June.

'You're sure don't look OK,' Sparrow grinned. 'Here. Try this.' He passed a mug over: it was a stiff whiskey.

'Just exactly what I need,' Coulter said.

He downed it, gasping as the liquor burned its way down his throat. It seemed to work and he began to feel better.

'I've got you some fresh clothes,' Sparrow continued. 'Ain't likely to be a good fit but I guess they'll do.'

When he had pulled on the clean clothes, Coulter followed Sparrow through to the main room where a number of firearms hung on the walls.

'Take your pick,' Sparrow said. 'We found the palomino, but I'm afraid Roberts got your guns. Here, take this pair of Colts.'

By the time June had rustled up some grub Coulter was beginning to feel a lot better.

'There are six of us,' he commented.

'Seven,' June interposed. 'I can handle a gun.'

'OK,' Coulter conceded. 'Seven of us. How many

do you think Roberts will bring?'

'There were a dozen or more of them out there,' Bragg said. 'They were coming this way and I don't think they were expecting much resistance. Now they know better they'll have every man they can get.'

'And how many do you reckon that would be?' Sparrow repeated.

'We can't be sure. Twice that many at least, maybe more.'

'Not good odds,' Sparrow said.

'Good enough,' Harrison put in.

'Yeah. We'll be ready for them.'

'What's been done?' Coulter asked.

'Don't worry, they'll get a warm reception,' Sparrow replied. 'We're well armed and we've got all the provisions we need. Harrison and me will station ourselves on the roof – should be able to pick off a few of them from up there and then lower ourselves though the skylight if things get a bit hot. We've assigned firing positions all around the place to cover most angles. Everyone knows what they have to do.'

'Might be an idea if someone takes up position outside the yard. That way he could come on them unexpectedly from behind,' Coulter observed.

'We're a bit stretched, but it sounds good,' Sparrow replied. 'Logan, you OK about that?'

'No problem.'

Coulter turned to Sparrow. 'It's mighty thin but it's

the best we can do.'

'Wish we had just a few more,' Jameson said.

'Yes, but it could be worse. Pity Roberts has got more of an idea what to expect now, but I think he'll still be in for a surprise.'

Sparrow turned to June. 'I'm still not too happy about you being involved in all this.' Then he turned to the company in general.

'What do you think? There's still time even now for June to ride out of here and get back to town.'

There was a pause. The men looked at each other. Any further discussion of the matter was cut short by June.

'You're not getting me away from here,' she said. 'I was brought up to take care of myself and handle a gun so let's hear no more of it.'

Sparrow still looked undecided but saw that June was adamant.

'I think I'd rather try bustin' a wild bronc than argue with you,' he finally laughed.

They had finished eating and no one needed to remind them that Roberts and his riders could arrive at any time. Purposefully, they took to their stations, checking their weapons one more time. June was assigned to cover the back of the house where the two bedrooms were situated.

'Keep your heads well down,' Coulter reminded them.

He and Bragg took their stations in the front room

which overlooked the yard where the main focus of attack would inevitably come. Sparrow and Harrison took to the low roof. Jameson was assigned a roving role, to cover wherever the pressure seemed heaviest. They settled down to wait.

Time passed. Coulter became aware of a clock on the mantelpiece ticking away the minutes. There were sounds of scuffling from up on the roof as Sparrow and Harrison settled into their positions. The glass in the windows had been knocked out and the shutters almost closed, allowing just enough space to see what was happening outside and for the barrel of a rifle to be pushed through the gap. Coulter had a clear view of the yard except for a corner to his left. Bragg at the other window had a view of this and between them they had the area covered. The minutes passed. Coulter looked across at Bragg. He appeared to be well enough recovered from his wounds. Coulter turned back to observe the yard. There was something ominous about its silence and emptiness. Suddenly there was a shout from the roof.

'Get ready! They're comin'!'

Coulter fingered the trigger of his shotgun. The silence seemed even more ominous, but it did not last for long. Presently Coulter's ears picked up a low rumbling sound. It grew louder, the galloping hoofs of a large body of horsemen. It seemed to go on for a long time, and then there came another sound, the crack of rifle fire. There was a response from outside and then from the rooftop. Coulter still could not see anything, but instantly the yard erupted into a thunder of noise. Roberts's men were firing, but it was a random volley. Smoke began to billow through the yard, and through it Coulter could now see them still coming forward but reining in their horses, surprised by the fusillade from the rooftop.

There was confusion out in the yard, and Coulter took advantage of it by firing into the melee of horses and riders. The nine-balls-to-the-cartridge charge wreaked havoc in the confined space. He saw three men lifted from their mounts, and then there came a burst of fire from Bragg and another rider toppled to the ground. Some of the riders were turning their horses; others had slid from their saddles to take refuge behind whatever cover they could find. Others continued running or dropped to the ground and sought to roll away. There were further reports from the rooftop. Roberts's men were firing back more accurately now. Bullets slapped into the walls of the waystation and Coulter pulled back his head as lead ripped into the window shutter, showering him with sharp fragments of wood. The clock which had been ticking on the mantelpiece shattered as a bullet ricocheted into the room. Coulter levered off another round. Bodies were littering the ground outside. Coulter reckoned there must be at least seven or eight of them. The rest of Roberts's men were in retreat, firing randomly as they sought to escape the killing ground of the yard. The firing was more sporadic and then it died away completely.

'OK back there?' Coulter yelled.

'We're fine!' Jameson replied.

Coulter looked across at Bragg. 'Caught them off guard,' he said. 'They'll be back, but they'll be more careful now.'

There was a scraping and clumping overhead. Coulter swung his Army Colt round but it was only Sparrow and Harrison coming down from the roof.

'Well done!' Sparrow said. 'We've given them somethin' to think about.' He was excited and it showed in his demeanour.

'You know,' Coulter said, 'I think you're almost enjoying it.'

'Ain't been in a scrap like this since the war,' Sparrow replied.

Coulter smiled then took another look out the window. Apart from the dead and dying in the yard, he could see no sign of anyone. He had certainly seen nothing as yet of Roberts himself. Coulter guessed he was out there somewhere, but he was too wily to put himself in the firing line. As if in answer to his thoughts, a voice suddenly called out, cutting through the echoing silence.

'Coulter!'

Sparrow looked at Coulter. There was a pause, and then the voice rang out again.

'Coulter!'

'Sounds to me like Roberts,' Coulter said.

Sparrow walked to the window where Bragg was still crouched.

'Is that you, Roberts?' he shouted. 'If so we ain't got nothin' to say to you.'

'I've got no quarrel with you,' Roberts called. 'Just send out Coulter and the rest of you can go free.'

'Go to hell, Roberts!'

'Don't be stupid. You haven't got a chance. We've got the place surrounded. All we want is Coulter.'

Sparrow looked at Coulter and a grin spread across his features.

'We've sure got them rattled,' he said. 'I don't think any of this was on Roberts's agenda.' He turned back to the window. 'If you want Coulter, you'd better come and get him.'

'This is the last chance you're gonna get. Send Coulter out now. He's a wanted man. We're just carrying out our duties as citizens. You don't want to get on the wrong side of the law.'

'Like I say, come right on in. We'll be waitin' for you.'

'I'll give you fifteen minutes. If Coulter's not outside with his hands in the air by that time we're comin' in to take him.'

Silence descended again.

'I reckon they're stallin' for time,' Coulter said. 'Sparrow, take my place. I'm going to take a look on the roof.'

Quickly they followed his instructions. Coulter swung himself up through a skylight on to the roof. It wasn't quite flat and had a slight camber and was protected by a projecting low wall. Keeping himself down, Coulter clambered to the back and then lifted his head to survey the scene. He was right. He could see some of Roberts's men moving through the brush towards the back of the house. They were being careless. One of them must have seen some movement on the roof for a shot came whining over Coulter's head. Raising his Colt, Coulter drew a bead on the gunman and squeezed the trigger. It was a difficult shot, but he saw the man fling up his arms and sink to the grass. He fired off another shot but didn't wait to see whether he had hit his target as rifle fire began to crack and more lead came whistling overhead. He slithered back to the skylight and lowered himself down.

'They're circling us,' he rapped.

Just then there came another rattle of gunfire from further away.

'Logan,' Sparrow said. 'Still doin' a job out there.'

'I guess he knows how to take care of himself,' Jameson added.

They had resumed their places by the windows and this time they didn't have long to wait. When the shooting started, it came from all sides, a furious cannonade that seemed to shake the waystation to its foundations. Bullets came screaming in, shattering objects to smithereens before embedding themselves in the walls and ceiling. With a cry Bragg fell back from the window, blood spurting from a shoulder wound. Coulter made to crawl across, but Bragg waved him aside.

'It's OK,' he gasped. 'It's only a flesh wound.'

To back his assertion he struggled to his feet and began pumping bullets into the yard outside, firing where he saw flame.

'We're wastin' lead,' Sparrow shouted. 'Hold your fire. Keep down.'

They lay flat as a fresh burst of fire rained upon the waystation.

'We need to do something,' Coulter called. 'They've got us pinned down.'

'The horses!' Bragg shouted. 'Why don't we loose the mustangs?'

Coulter looked at Sparrow.

'It might work,' Coulter said. 'The horses will take some of them out. It could give us the chance to break free.'

'Problem is, how do we let them out? There's open ground between us and the corral.'

'Can't be helped,' Coulter said. 'I reckon it's our best chance. I'm willing to give it a go. If most of you take the back rooms and give me covering fire, I might make it.'

'No!' June intervened. 'Coulter, it's too big a chance.'

'It's no more risky than some of the other things we've had to do,' he said, trying to comfort her. 'I've been in worse situations than this and come through.'

'Let me go,' Sparrow said. 'I'm gettin' too old anyway.'

'No!' Coulter snapped. 'This is my quarrel.'

'But—' June began, when Coulter cut her short.

'No more buts. We're wastin' time. Now let's just do it.'

There was a moment's silence. Sparrow looked at Coulter as though he was about to say something further, then shook his head.

'Right,' Coulter said. 'Let's take up position out back. Bragg, are you sure you're all right to stay and cover here?'

Bragg's face was creased and blanched, but he had managed to staunch the bleeding with a rag.

'Go ahead,' he replied. 'Give 'em hell.'

The rest of them made their way to the back of the building, taking care to keep low. Roberts and his men seemed to have taken a break. They had no reason to rush things, Coulter reflected. They must consider that they could take their time. When everybody had taken their places in order to provide the best possible covering fire, Coulter moved to the door.

'As soon as I open the door, start firing,' he said.

The others nodded their assent. Coulter checked

that his Colts were loaded and ready. Holding one in his right hand, he nodded his head and then flung open the door. Instantly there came a deafening crescendo of gunfire as the people in the waystation let loose with a raking curtain of hot lead. Coulter, doubled up, was running as hard as he could across the open space. For a moment there was no response as Roberts' men, taken by surprise, tried to grasp what was happening.

Coulter was now halfway across the gap. The horses in the corral were plunging and snorting in fright and terror. Some of them were already down. Then Roberts's men began to fire in return. Even now some of them had failed to register that Coulter was on his way to the corral. They were firing back at the relay station whose walls were bursting and exploding as bullets tore into them. Fortunately they were well built. Now Roberts's gunmen had seen Coulter and some of them began to fire in his direction. He felt the wind of bullets flying past. He bent over further. Bullets tore into the earth around him. As he ran plumes of flame leaped from his gun as he fired randomly at possible places of concealment. His legs pumping as fast as he could make them, he was almost at the gate of the corral. Hen he felt something sear his arm and the gun fell from his hand. Gasping for breath he reached the corral and flung himself at the gate.

The frantic horses inside were neighing and frothing in fear and milling about in their confusion. Bullets now ripped into them but Coulter had the bolt withdrawn. He pushed against the gate. For a worried moment he thought the pressure of horseflesh might prevent it opening, but once it had gained momentum it swung wide and the frenzied mustangs began to surge towards the exit. Coulter's concern now was not with bullets but with avoiding the flying hoofs. Desperately he rolled to one side and kept rolling. Fortunately he was partially protected by the open gate. The panicking horses were running free. At first they charged straight ahead but confronted by the wall of the waystation, began to spread out in other directions. Coulter was protected from gunfire to some extent by the charging herd. Getting to his feet and pulling the other gun from its holster he began to run back towards the building, avoiding horses which had strayed in that direction. Taking shelter behind the angle of the wall, he began to loose off shots, trying to avoid hitting any of the animals.

'Let's go!' he shouted.

Immediately the door was flung open and the others, led by Sparrow, charged out, firing as they tried picking out where the gunslicks were concealed. It was difficult to fire accurately through the mad mêlée, but in the main they were sheltered by the careering herd. All was confusion. The air was thick with dust and smoke and the acrid smell of gunpowder. Guns cracked, horses brayed and hoofs thundered. Mingled with these came a new sound, a howling and screaming as Roberts's gunhawks began to fall under the trampling hoofs of the charging horses. They had been taken by surprise. Confused and disorientated, some of them were running straight into the path of the semi-wild horses, others were running in disarray to try and seek out their own mounts and escape any way they could. They were making themselves targets.

Coulter was running along the side of the waystation and emerging at a corner, began shooting in support of Bragg. He was out of ammunition and, as he stopped firing became aware for the first time that he had been hit. With the realization came the shock of pain searing across his left arm from which blood was oozing. The arm swung uselessly. He sank to the ground, a spectator now of what was happening all around. As he lay, he became aware of somebody near him. He turned painfully to see Roberts standing over him with a rifle in his hands.

'Coulter, I want to see the look in your eyes when you die.'

Coulter was helpless. Roberts's men might have paid the price, but Roberts was still alive to hire more gunhawks and re-establish himself. Everything Coulter had done to thwart him might prove to have been in vain. Slowly, Roberts raised the gun.

'You've caused me a lot of trouble, Coulter. Now

I'm going to blow the top of your head clean off.'

The look in Roberts's eyes was like moonlight on cold water. Slowly his finger closed around the trigger. Then there was a sudden movement behind him and for the fraction of a second Roberts was distracted.

'Coulter!' a voice called. It was the voice of June Campbell.

Roberts made a slight movement in the direction of the sound and, as he did so, Coulter swung his left leg, catching Roberts on the shin. The gun exploded but Roberts was off balance and the shot crashed into the wall of the building. Wincing with pain, Coulter threw himself upwards, his head thudding into Roberts's midriff. Roberts tried to bring the gun around, but he was winded and, as he crumpled, Coulter delivered another blow to the stomach with his good arm. Roberts swung the gun and caught Coulter a glancing blow across the head which brought him to his knees, rendering him almost unconscious.

Struggling to regain his senses, Coulter became aware through waves of pain and darkness that Roberts was running to make his escape, but as he broke blindly into the open it was straight into the path of a couple of charging crazed mustangs. He was bowled over like a rag doll, screaming as their hoofs trampled him into the ground. Behind the horses came others, stomping him down into a bloody mess of crushed bone and gore. The horses were plunging on but now the rattle of gunfire was getting less. Then it became random and subsided altogether. The herd was disappearing into the distance, but many horses lay on the ground, some thrashing but others unmoving. Among them and distributed about the yard were the bodies of gunmen either shot or mangled underfoot.

Coulter felt himself being lifted, and when he raised his eyes it was to see June looking down at him.

'Coulter,' she kept repeating. 'Coulter.'

He lay in her arms and managed to smile up at her.

'June,' he murmured, 'looks like we won.'

The others stood as if bewildered now by the roaring silence which succeeded the furore of battle. Some were exposed and realizing this, dropped to the ground or took what shelter they could. Moments passed, moments that seemed to extend to minutes. Then Sparrow, who had taken cover behind a water trough, broke the silence.

'Coulter!' he called. 'Are you OK?'

Coulter lifted his head. 'I'm OK!' he called back. 'I'm hit but it's only my arm. What about the rest of you?'

The others began to respond. They were still nervous, unsure whether any of the gunslicks remained, but there was no further firing. Bragg came over to where Coulter lay in June's embrace and made to assist her in lifting him up, but Coulter held out his hand and with a little help from June, struggled to his feet himself.

'I don't think we'll be having any more trouble from Roberts,' he said, indicating where the mangled body lay in the fading sunlight.

They gathered together back in the waystation. Apart from Bragg and Coulter, Logan had also been hit. Otherwise there were no losses other than to the horses. Outside, the yard was a scene of carnage.

'I guess we got off pretty light,' Sparrow commented.

Later, Jameson rode out to fetch a doctor and the undertaker from Green Gulch. In the meantime June, with a little help from the others who were unhurt, did what she could to assist the wounded. By late evening most of the remaining mustangs had been rounded up and the place largely cleared. Night descended with its healing balm. Coulter and June stood outside the waystation as the sun disappeared over the rim of the western prairie.

'What are you going to do now?' June said.

'I don't know.'

Coulter looked down at the woman by his side. He wanted to tell her how he felt but he felt a return of the old awkwardness. She was not like any other woman he had known and the feelings she evoked were new and unfamiliar.

'Guess I'll go back to prospectin',' he replied lamely.

They stood in silence for a few moments till Coulter heard a sound behind him and turned to find Harrison.

'Sure is a fine night,' the rancher commented as he approached them. Coulter nodded in agreement as Harrison came up alongside.

'You know, I couldn't help overhearin' what you just said, about goin' back to prospectin' that is,' Harrison remarked. 'But if you'd be interested I got a better idea.'

Coulter looked puzzled. 'Yeah? What's that?'

'Now that this is over I'm gonna need a heap of support to rebuild the Block H. And once I get it back on its feet, I'm gonna need help to run the place.'

Coulter glanced sideways at June and their eyes met.

'How about it, Coulter?' Harrison said. 'There's a job waitin' for you.'

Coulter hesitated.

'Stay,' June said. 'Besides, you're going to need time for those wounds to heal.'

Coulter didn't know what to say. He felt confused.

'What about Bragg?' he said. 'We've been ridin' together for a long time.'

At that moment the frame of the big man appeared in the doorway of the waystation, his arm in a sling.

'I already signed up,' he said.

Coulter looked across at him and then they both laughed.

'Then I guess I just signed to the Block H brand too,' Coulter replied.

Grinning, Harrison turned away and in a moment the door closed on him and Bragg. Coulter looked at June. Her eyes were warm and pellucid in the gathering starlight.

'Don't say anything,' she whispered.

Taking her in his arms, Coulter held her close and then their lips met. Watching from the window of the waystation, Bragg turned to the others.

'Reckon Coulter finally got over that dog,' he said.